A CHIMERA'S REVENGE

EVE LANGLAIS

Chimera Secrets 4 - Romantic Horror

PROLOGUE

"Freak. Look at him twitching."

"Is he even allowed to be at school with us normal kids?"

The evil taunts had long since lost their ability to hurt. Adrian knew what the other children saw when they looked at him. Saw it himself every day in the mirror. He wished it was different, but the motor neuron disease attacking his body had no remorse. The degeneration of the nerves that controlled his muscles made it impossible at times to do the simplest tasks. Yet, in the ultimate cruelty, motor neuron diseased, MND, left his mind intact so that he could remember what it used to be like, before the tremors started then the first paralyzing time a limb didn't work as expected.

"He's the load his mother should have swallowed," snickered another bully.

The world was a cruel place, and Benedict, star of

the football team, led the way when it came to bullying, especially those he considered inferior. A word Adrian was pretty sure Benedict couldn't spell.

"Leave him alone." The dulcet voice of an angel came to his rescue.

"Are you seriously protecting him?" Benedict drawled with a roll of his eyes. "Look at him. He's a fucking pussy. He can't even defend himself."

"Exactly," snapped a pert female voice. "I can't believe you're bullying him. Pick on someone who can at least fight back."

A rescue with an insult, probably not intentional, but it still had the ability to sting. *I'd defend myself if I could.* But Benedict wasn't the type to be swayed by words.

"You got the hots for the freak, Jane?"

"Of course not." He could hear the shock in the retort.

Adrian couldn't blame her for the disgust. His own mother couldn't handle his situation. She dumped him the moment he got inconvenient. Now he got government-mandated care, which didn't amount to much. Lucky for him, he had foster parents who actually gave a damn about his well-being.

"I wonder if he gets boners." Benedict strode over with that rolling-hip lankiness that the athletic all possessed. "Hey, freak. Does your dick still work?"

The question might have cowed someone else; however, Adrian had been living inside imaginary worlds for a long time now. He'd read, listened, and watched so much that little shocked him.

Which was why he could say, "Suck it and find out."

"You motherfucker." Hands reached for him, grasping his shirt and hauling him forward.

Jane threw herself between them and shoved at her boyfriend. "Are you nuts? Put him down. You can't beat up the kid in the wheelchair. They'll expel you. And you know the recruiters are coming next week."

The magic words that got Benedict—looking for a scholarship ride as a quarterback—to slam Adrian back into his seat.

Benedict glared. "Get out of my way, freak." He strutted past, but Jane hesitated, biting her lower lip and glancing at Adrian.

"Are you okay?" she asked.

She'd talked to him and come to his aid. He was better than okay.

"He's a shithead," Adrian said, trying for suave but sounding more like a croaking frog.

"Yup."

"So why date him?"

She glanced at the receding backside of the wide athlete and shrugged. "He's hot."

"He's an idiot."

Oddly enough, she didn't rise to Benedict's defense. She glanced at Adrian. "I should go."

The first time they'd met and actually talked. But

not the last time. He and Jane ran into each other almost daily after that. Each time, she stopped and spoke to him, even smiled and laughed. Told him he was too smart for his own good.

Was it any wonder he fell in love with her? And his hatred for Benedict grew. Not only did that asshole keep bullying Adrian, he got the girl.

But he didn't get the last laugh. Adrian had his revenge. And lived to regret it.

CHAPTER ONE

Time for me to exit the scene and wipe all traces.

Adrian had started with the clinic he'd grown from the ground down. Literally. The facility that cost him billions to build in secret—and greased more hands than he realized worked in government—went deep under the earth, hiding from the world his incredible progress when it came to fixing humanity, which some would claim was a lost cause.

Some days he agreed, and with the loss of the Chimaeram Clinic, humanity might very well be screwed when it came to their next stage of evolution.

The Earth was going into a radical shift, and people needed to change with it or die. It sounded noble when Cerberus used that line on the guys who funded his very expensive lab. The real truth was Adrian liked being a scientist, the madder, the better.

But a true scientist needed a lab, and his was gone now, destroyed by his command. Adrian Chimera was about to disappear from the world.

At least for now.

Being a cutting-edge scientist with a vision meant being careful to not reveal plans too early lest the less enlightened not understand his end goal.

Improving humanity. Curing the sick. Healing the maimed. Giving everyone another chance. Some ingrates didn't appreciate what he did. Word was out about the secret lab in the mountains. He'd evacuated but not before taking casualties.

His main doctor, Aloysius Cerberus, was still missing. As were some of the projects, lost during the transfer from the secret lab in the Rockies to the new facility hidden in the northern parts of Alberta, where the woods spread as far as the eye could see. A helicopter transporting one of his more precious patients went down not long after taking off. It, and its three passengers, had yet to be located.

He hoped they stayed hidden. The last thing he needed was for any of his missing patients to emerge in a public place. Their appearance would raise questions and probably get him arrested.

Laws could be pesky things that way.

Luckily, before his last lab was destroyed, he managed to upload all his files to a secure server—along with the missing Dr. Cerberus's notes. It made Adrian sad to destroy a place where he'd accomplished so much; however, the clinic wasn't safe anymore.

Someone found out what he was doing. *My enemies are closing in.*

They're coming to get you, his inner voice cackled.

Time to disappear for a while.

Which meant ridding himself of his other home. The penthouse condo with its view of the city, two-story windows opening onto a panorama that could take the breath away at sunset. There were rooms sectioned off from the main living area. Guest room, exercise, master bedroom, of course, and den. Plus, Jane's room.

Jane lived in a suite to rival his own. The view from it breathtaking. The machinery hooked to her very expensive.

And yet no amount of money in the world, no treatment, no fervent cursing could fix her. Jane was in what they rudely termed a vegetative state.

Entering her room, weariness hit him. How many times had he visited in the past few years? Less as time passed and she didn't so much as twitch an eyelid. When he'd first started treating her, he'd had such hope. That hope slowly dwindled to the point he now pondered the unthinkable.

He grabbed her hand, noticing the fine porcelain of it. More than two decades in a coma had left it smooth. No callouses from life. He rubbed his thumb over the limp fingers. Slightly cold to the touch. There had been issues of late with maintaining her body temperature.

"I don't suppose you'll wake up in the next five minutes?" Because it wouldn't take him long to grab what he wanted and get out of here.

Jane didn't move, a sleeping beauty who'd grown from girl to woman while in her coma. Another tragedy when it came to the use of drugs among teens. She was considered the lucky one, given her boyfriend, Benedict, died the night they both ingested lethal dope.

Machines kept Jane alive at the wish of her parents. But when they passed on, the hospital made plans to pull her plug. Having kept tabs on her, Adrian found out about her upcoming fate. Remembering the girl who'd saved him on the schoolyard, Adrian made arrangements to have Jane picked up from the hospital. The paperwork on her move was lost. Her location unknown to everyone but him.

Alone with her in his condo, her room converted into a mini lab, he'd done his best to fix the first woman he'd crushed on. Failed despite his best efforts. Her brain had yet to show a bleep. She still required a tube to breathe.

Which might have been a mercy. The cure wasn't a boon to everyone. For some, it made things worse.

And you would know, boyo.

In Jane's case, while he managed to heal her body, her mind was obviously too far-gone. He'd done his best to bring her to life, giving her a blend of animal DNA, from the avian to preserve her fine-boned nature to a lizard, which could heal amputated limbs. Even an echidna, to give her an ability to fall into a state of torpor, where the body basically hibernated.

It seemed to work. She was perfect. Her muscles didn't atrophy, all injuries healed, but she didn't absorb or produce any heat, and her circulation remained sluggish. Her brain showed no sign of activity. Not even a teeny tiny blip.

Adrian sighed as he stared at her perfect features. A sleeping princess who never woke up.

Maybe if I gave her a kiss... Not the first time he'd thought of it, yet he'd never acted on it. There was something about touching a woman who couldn't say yes that held him back. But this wasn't about desire. This was saying goodbye.

There was nothing sexual in the kiss he placed on her forehead but so much regret. A man who'd not cried in years, Adrian couldn't stop it. One hot tear fell onto her skin. "I'm sorry, Jane." Sorry for so many things.

Sorry doesn't fix it.

Shut up.

What's wrong, boyo? Does the truth hurt?

As a matter of fact, it did, and nostalgia made him procrastinate. She wasn't waking up, and he wasted time. His enemies might have discovered he'd returned. He shouldn't tarry. It was time to let Jane go. To maybe let a lot of his dreams go before he created any more nightmares.

He sighed as he stood. It took but a second to flick a few switches, to hear the constant whup and whoosh of the air compressor stop, the lack of noise jarring.

To his surprise, her chest continued to rise and fall. Probably a delayed reaction.

He stared at her one last time as he whispered, "Good night, my sweet Jane."

It took a resolve of cold steel to not look back as he left the room. Even once he grabbed his emergency satchel—with passport, credit cards, and cash—from his safe, he was tempted to go back in one last time.

What if she was still alive?

What if she wasn't?

When would he accept the fact the Jane he crushed on in high school was gone?

He left without peeking again. The Town Car waited for him at the curb when he exited, Jett having pulled up just a moment before.

He slammed the door shut, and Jett immediately pulled away.

Only then did Adrian dial a number on his phone. When the other end answered, he entered a sequence of digits. Then hung up.

The car was almost three blocks away when an explosion ripped the sky behind them, and he hunched in the seat, closing his eyes, the pain of losing not only his home but the woman he'd love for so long intense.

The news reported the next day that the penthouse of his building was gone. The entire level collapsed into the floor underneath it—the occupants luckily away for the evening. A smoldering ruin that would take days to sift through. No known casualties yet. But Jane was in there somewhere and would be found.

Questions would be asked.

Adrian planned to be long gone by then.

CHAPTER TWO

ADRIAN'S NEW HOME IN THE WOODS LACKED THE hustle and bustle of the city. It also lacked the services of a live-in chef—a treat he missed from his defunct clinic.

Just me, myself, and the voices in my head. More than one now, a few not actually saying anything coherent, more like feelings, thoughts.

Bad thoughts. They wanted him to do things. Bad things. Adrian hadn't used to be a violent man; however, there was something cathartic about smashing things.

And when it came to killing...There was a euphoria in snuffing life that compared to nothing else.

Maybe that's what I need. To kill something.

The insidious suggestion had him slamming the tumbler on the glass panel railing running the perimeter of his outdoor balcony. Amber liquid sloshed over the rim, and he grimaced.

What a waste. He needed the numbing effect. Ever since he'd left his condo burning more than a week ago, his life had gone to shit.

First off, his new secret lab? The one he'd squirreled everyone to? The facility that was not prepared for the influx? The projects revolted the second night there and broke out. Not too many people survived their passage—on either side.

So many dead and the cost to hide the damage? More zeroes than he liked. Cleanup crews didn't come cheap, and yet you couldn't be a mad scientist without one.

Adrian tossed back the expensive booze. Nothing but the best for him. Now at least. Having a second chance at life meant he tried to savor everything he could. Food. Fleshly pleasures. The softest fabrics for his clothes. The most expensive alcohol.

He didn't scrimp when it came to luxuries. The thing was their enjoyment proved fleeting. The loneliness, however, remained constant.

The view behind his house was a nature lover's dream. The fir trees remained green, even this time of year. The first snow had come and melted, but the true brunt of winter was yet to come. Only a few weeks until Christmas. His first alone in...too many years to count. He'd never thought before of his clinic with all its staff as family but now sorely felt their loss.

Slipping the tumbler onto a glass-topped table, he dropped his robe, not worried about his nudity. There weren't any neighbors around for miles. He headed for the hot tub on the deck, the heat causing steam to rise in the cool night air. He'd bought this place a while ago, using shell companies to hide his ownership. His backup in case everything else went to hell. A good thing he'd planned ahead. He needed to be prepared more than ever now that some of his greatest creations were at large.

He turned his back to the forest as he sat on the edge of the tub and dipped his feet in. The hot water eased the muscles of his calves, and the steam rising from the surface helped reduce some of the chill invading his skin. He already had a large fluffy towel sitting folded on the edge for when he emerged.

A rustling sound caught his attention. Not uncommon this close to the woods. Sometimes even the smallest of rodents could sound like a rampaging beast.

Probably only a squirrel.

He slipped into the water, uttering a happy sigh. The heat eased right into his rigid frame, and he closed his eyes as he leaned his head back to relax.

Rustle. Crinkle. Crunch.

Whatever approached didn't even try to hide. He kept his head tilted back and eyes closed. Ignored the scratch of claws on wood.

Let it climb to the deck.

The stench of it rolled over him. The pungent aroma of something that had forgotten how to bathe but hadn't regressed enough to realize it had to groom itself. A basic animal thing that all his feral patients seemed to forget.

Is that when I should worry? When he couldn't stand the smell of himself?

The thing huffed, and he imagined it steamed the air, its rage almost a palpable heat.

"And here we thought it was the clinic drawing them," he mused aloud. Adrian opened his eyes and beheld one of his lost patients.

It was male, very far-gone. His feral nature had completely taken over. His hair was a gnarled mess that tied into his bird's nest of a beard. His eyes were a baleful amber, glaring at Adrian sullenly. The claws on his hands long, yellow, and curved. Much like the sloth he'd been mixed with.

"Hello, Christopher." Adrian might have assigned all his pets numerical identifications when they came into the clinic, but that didn't mean he forgot their names. He knew them all. Even the dead ones.

No recognition lit his gaze. Rather the hybrid formally known as Christopher opened his mouth wide and honked. Not exactly the noise expected. Possibly why the man lost the battle. The more animals added to the mix, the more a host had to fight to remain on top.

It could be done. He had pets who'd gone on to do well. Like Luke, the bastard who'd escaped.

But he'll be back. They always came back.

"Are you alone, Christopher?" Adrian didn't dare move his gaze from the threat. Because he didn't for one minute harbor any foolish thoughts about what Christopher wanted to do.

The returning patients only ever seemed to want one thing.

"Care to join me?" He gestured to the water.

Blargh. The thing advanced, a strangely jolting walk on two legs that wobbled almost spaghetti-like.

"You never did say if you came alone." Because Christopher was one of those who'd recently escaped. "Was it you that figured out how to open the locks?" An impressive feat, given the patients were placed in glass-like cubes with holes only for ventilation. Nothing big enough for a limb. Yet they'd all escaped.

Christopher gripped onto the hot tub and finally went to all fours, clinging to the edge, wary of the bubbling water.

"You should have run away," Adrian said sadly with a shake of his head. He didn't understand why only some of those who escaped succeeded. Why, oh why was he a lodestone for their return?

Christopher leaped. In a smooth motion, Adrian pulled himself from the water, drew the gun hidden under the towel folded by the side, and shot the hybrid.

The body hit the water, which immediately

foamed red. So much for further soaking. The tub would need to be drained. Adrian poured another glass of whiskey before he dialed.

When the other end answered he said, "I require a cleanup."

"Another one?" the voice replied.

Second one this week. And still seventeen projects on the run.

CHAPTER THREE

"I THINK YOU BETTER CHECK THE NEWS," JETT declared the moment Adrian opened the door for him the next day. He'd first checked his cameras, his paranoia starting to get the best of him. The slightest sound made him twitch.

"Why would I watch the news?" Adrian asked with a roll of his eyes. He'd lost interest in politics when it became a party-line-split fight on every issue. As for the weather, a finger stuck outside was more accurate than those imbeciles.

"You need to watch, because I think the media found someone."

"If one of my missing patients is making waves and getting caught on camera then they won't be loose for long." The men in the black suits would be along to subdue them in short order.

"Yeah, I know that, but I think when you see who it

is, you'll want to catch this one yourself." Jett knew where the television was. His right-hand man—and only friend—visited almost daily to check on him. Funny how Adrian used to want someone around to protect him at all times and now relied on himself. Killing quieted the voices for a little bit.

"Do you know who it is?" Adrian asked, sinking onto the couch.

"Yup. But you're not going to believe it."

Jett changed the channel and found the local news station playing a commercial of course.

While a car zipped in the background showing someone fancy driving in a way contrary to laws and regulations, Jett grabbed a water from the fridge.

"How is your wife?" Adrian asked. Jett and Becky hadn't known each other long; however, they'd bonded. Deeply. Especially after she became a hybrid mermaid. The marriage came after she got pregnant and the hormones kicked in. Who knew having tadpoles in her belly would make her so emotional?

Poor Jett had a preacher flown out the same day he caught her crying by the lake about being an unwed mother and their children being born bastards.

Adrian got to be the best man, which a shocker. And Cerberus gave Becky away.

It had to be the strangest wedding in history, especially since Becky spent it with her feet submerged in a tub of water.

The commercial flipped and screamed about how insurance was screwing him out of his money.

Jett ignored it. "Becky's good. But she's getting some weird fucking cravings."

"It's normal. All pregnant women get them."

"Chocolate-covered flies or grasshoppers would be normal. Live frogs are not."

Adrian blinked at the news. "I thought she liked her meat well done."

"Not anymore." Said grimly.

Interesting. He'd have to check and see what aquatic strain she carried in her DNA. Appetite regression was uncommon in those maintaining their human façade.

The news logo flashed on screen, and Jett turned, raising the sound as the announcer came on.

"A blazing inferno on Main Street was thought to have a casualty today when a woman was seen walking into the burning building."

The image on screen changed to a shaky video of a burning brownstone, the flames billowing from the windows. The smoke pouring into the sky. From the crowd a woman appeared.

Stark naked.

Even without the nudity, she was striking. Her hair long was auburn with a hint of curl. Her flesh like fine porcelain and laid bare to everyone's view. The shapely woman paid no one any mind as she walked straight into the burning building.

The announcer returned. "That woman never exited, and moments later, there was an explosion." The view changed once more to the building. *Kaboom.* *"Jesus. Bleep. Bleep. It blew up!"* The frantic yelling went with the shaky video displaying a building broken, the top of it shooting flames into the sky, a wider pan showing debris on the ground.

But Adrian didn't focus on the destruction. Instead he forced a whisper. "Is that..." He couldn't say it.

"Jane?" Jett shrugged. "Sure as fuck looks like her. But that's impossible. You said she was in the condo when it blew."

"She was." Adrian flung himself from the couch. "That can't be her. Did they find that woman's body?" Because they never did find Jane's when all the sifting was done.

"Nope. But—and here's where you might want to jump onto the internet—turns out this is the second time someone's seen a redhead around fires in the last week."

"It can't be her," muttered more to convince himself than Jett. Adrian fetched his laptop and began searching. The videos proved easy to find. Three in total it turned out. Three videos of a woman going into a burning structure, an explosion, no woman coming out.

Could it be her?

He studied the grainy images from every possible angle but never got a clear one of her face.

Jane or not, he had to get his hands on that woman.

Which was why he packed a bag later that day and, along with Jett, embarked on the long drive back to the city he'd just abandoned. Calgary, Alberta.

The scene and start of so many of his crimes. Accomplishments, too.

Back when he was still in a wheelchair, growing more and more dependent on aid every day, he used to study at a small college. A private facility that had long since shut its doors due to unethical practices.

Not his practices, he should add. Although, had they known what he and Cerberus did in their lab... It wasn't just the ethics boards that would have gotten involved.

But they never even suspected. That tiny college was where he first met Aloysius Cerberus. A South African scholar who'd fled his country's turmoil for a new life. A new chance.

With Aloysius's steady hands and quick grasp of biology and using Adrian's brain, they created the first remedy.

An utter failure. The mouse they gave it to died in minutes. As did the next dozen after that, despite all the tweaks. And yet, they didn't get discouraged.

Well, Aloysius didn't. Adrian, though, was desperate.

"I don't understand why it's not working." Adrian *couldn't pace. Hell, he could barely hold a damn spoon anymore. His time was ticking.*

"*Their bodies keep rejecting the tweaks on the chromosome strings. We need a better delivery system.*" It was Aloysius that gave Adrian his light bulb moment.

Rather than try and modify existing broken genes, Adrian chose another route. Introducing new genes, already existing animal ones. The delivery system a secret he'd concocted. Aloysius was his hands.

And they finally had their first success. Kind of. The mouse with paralysis regained the use of its limbs.

Meanwhile Adrian lost the ability to move his arms.

"*Give it to me,*" Adrian begged Aloysius.

"*I can't. It's still in the testing phase. We haven't yet studied any possible side effects.*"

Adrian didn't give a fuck. He was degrading fast now. "*Please. Help me.*"

A good thing Cerberus was as in love with the science as he was. He injected Adrian. The pain proved incredible.

Aloysius catalogued it all, especially the fact Adrian not only regained control of his hands but his legs, too. Adrian kept on taking small doses, then larger ones, getting more confident with each injection.

He became living proof that the cure worked.

But, like many medications on the market, there were side effects.

CHAPTER FOUR

"THE BOSS IS FUCKING NUTS," JETT CONFIDED TO his wife when he called her that night from his room adjoining the luxury suite Chimera had booked for their stay.

"That nut job is the only person that might be able to help me when our babies come, so don't let him get killed."

Legend might claim mermaids were also sirens, luring men with their beautiful voices. In Becky's case, it was a deadly promise. His gentle Red had turned fiery.

And he liked it.

"You'll be fine." Something Jett prayed for every day. He just hoped someone actually listened, because in the case of the people he killed... Yeah...they never got rescued.

"I heard from Jayda today." Cerberus's daughter

had formed a bond with Becky and kept in touch.

"Any news about her father?"

"Still missing. But some idiot tried to go after her again. Marcus apparently ate him."

"Jeezus." Jett rubbed the bridge of his nose. "Hope he didn't get indigestion."

Becky giggled. The only sound in the world he lived for. "I think I didn't chew a frog good enough the other day, and it wiggled going down."

"It's a good thing I love you, Red." Because anyone else he'd have shot for being weird. "Other than your desire for Kermit, how you feeling?"

"Good. But I spent most of last night in the pool."

Which had to be cold. The heater had died last week, and he was waiting for a part.

"Have you seen anyone loitering?" He'd left her guarded by a pair of guys he trusted, but given the recent kidnapping of Cerberus and his daughter, he worried. He wouldn't have come with Adrian if she hadn't insisted. Someone had to keep an eye on the one guy who could handle the babies in his wife's belly.

"I'm fine. My friends are watching out for me." Friends that refused to come near Jett because they were different, like his wife. Chimera didn't know about them. Jett thought of them as his secret leverage should things get difficult.

"I should only be gone for a few days." Long enough for Adrian to track down the chick who looked like Jane. Once upon a time, Jett would have said it was impossible for a girl in a coma to walk away from a condo that blew up. Then he met Adrian Chimera.

"What do you think Adrian will do if he finds her?"

What would any man do if he found the woman he'd crushed on for decades? "Hopefully get laid." Because the boss could stand to relax a bit.

"Jett!"

"What? It's the truth. He is seriously uptight these days. Ever since he lost the lab and all his patients, he's been acting weird."

"He's always been weird."

"How about weirder? I don't know if he's as in control as he likes to claim."

"It's a daily struggle." He could almost see Becky's shrug through the phone. "You still getting that coffee with your old friend later?"

"Might as well. We're both in town for once."

"Be careful."

"Never!" he exclaimed with a chuckle. "Call you later."

He hung up and checked on Dr. Chimera, who—no surprise—wasn't sleeping after all but on his phone. Jett pointed to his mouth, then his watch, and flashed ten fingers three times.

The boss nodded.

Half-hour would be all he needed.

The coffee shop was only two blocks away, and

when he walked in, Jett saw the person he was meeting right away. Sitting out in the open, brazen as could be.

Jett shook his head as he made his way toward him. "You know, if Chimera hears you're in town, he'll send out a team to take you in."

"I'd like to see him try." Luke didn't look bothered at all. The escaped patient appeared better than Jett had ever seen him. Tanned, healthy looking, with a full head of hair and a beard. Then again, what would you expect from an ex-patient the guards had nicknamed the wolfman?

"So why did you want to meet?" Jett asked. He still wasn't entirely sure how Luke got a hold of his number.

"I hear your wife's pregnant."

The words might have chilled Jett's blood, but he still slid into the chair opposite the man. "Twins. Twice the fun." Twice the guns if they were girls. Wasn't no boy going to be laying a hand on his princesses.

"Margaret is due any day now. I think." The mask slipped for a moment, and Jett saw the worry and fatigue pulling at Luke's features.

"How is that possible?" Margaret shouldn't have been more than five months or so along.

"Fucked if I know." Luke shrugged. "Needless to say, it puts us in a bit of a pickle."

Jett didn't believe in beating around the bush. He trampled it. "You want Chimera to help with the birth."

"I don't. At least I didn't, but..." Luke sighed and drummed his fingers. "She can't have the baby in a regular hospital. Heck, even having a midwife attend is too dangerous."

Because the child might not be human.

"You're too late. Maybe you didn't hear. Boss man doesn't have a clinic anymore."

"I know." Luke frowned. "I didn't expect them to attack."

Jett cast him a sharp glance. "What the fuck is that supposed to mean? You behind the shit that happened at the clinic?"

"Kind of."

"Explain." Jett leaned back and crossed his arms as he glared at the fucker who'd caused so much trouble. He'd told Adrian to shoot Luke back when he first started his shit. Boss should have listened.

"About two months after we escaped, Margaret got really sick."

"This is when you were living in the jungle?"

Luke's lips twisted. "Yeah. You were probably still monitoring us then."

"Boss was. But then he lost you."

That brought a smirk. "I never even knew he'd chipped me."

"How did you get rid of the tracker?"

"I didn't. I had help. See, Margaret caught a fever. I thought it was some weird tropical thing. But she began losing weight. I got worried and brought her to a doctor I found living in a remote part of jungle. Sven something or other. He was a biologist doing some kind of study. He had a full lab in his house."

Jett could see where this story was going. "You let a human doctor examine her."

"I didn't have a choice. Margaret was so sick." Luke's expression turned haunted, the memory clearly still bothering him. "I killed Sven once we figured out it was a vitamin problem. Not enough iron in her diet. What I didn't know was he apparently sent details about Margaret and me to someone else."

"Shit, you got captured."

Something akin to embarrassment flitted across his face. "I thought we'd be safe for a few days. There was food. A bed. Running water. All the comforts she'd been lacking. I just wanted her to get better. They arrived before we cleared out."

"Who did?"

"I don't know. A bunch of guys with guns. Because of Margaret, I couldn't fight. They took us prisoner."

"And you told them everything."

"Not at first." Luke stared at the tabletop, a man torn about something. "But they were good. The guy they sent in, he was so fucking nice and normal. He treated me and Maggie like gold. Like we were important. He was the one who told me about the trackers in our bodies. He used some kind of EMP pulse to deactivate them."

"You thought you could trust them." Jett's lip curled.

"No. I wasn't that stupid, but they used my worry about Maggie and the baby against me. They said something wasn't normal. But they couldn't help without knowing more. They said she needed a special doctor. Someone who understood what was happening in her body."

"You told them about the clinic."

Luke's gaze met his. Sharp and cold. "I didn't say shit about Chimera's fucking lab. Hell, I didn't say shit about what was done to me, but they knew. And they knew how to get me to talk. They stuck us in cages. They made Maggie cry."

Given how Jett felt when Becky sobbed, he could understand why Luke spilled his secrets. "How much did you reveal?"

"Not everything if that's what you're wondering. They already knew about us, though. Had Cerberus's name. Knew he was a doctor there."

"They kidnapped him when they attacked the clinic. We lost a lot of good men."

"Good is debatable. They were part of the secret."

"They were innocent."

"Cerberus and the other doctors aren't."

Jett canted his head. "Maybe not, but now he's gone. The clinic has been destroyed. Every single fucking patient is either dead or in hiding. And here you are. Why?"

"I told you why. I need Chimera."

"And I'm supposed to believe that?" Jett arched a brow. "You're a traitor. For all I know you called me here as part of a trap."

Luke sighed. "No trap. I need help."

Despite everything, Jett believed him. "Who are these people that caught you?" he asked.

"I don't know. I never got their names. I do know they seem to be Russian backed. But they obviously had connections, given how they've been moving around."

"How did you escape?"

A wave of green rolled over Luke's eyes. "By killing every single fucker who stood in my way. The night they went after Cerberus, they practically emptied out the place." Luke shrugged. "I knew I might never get a better chance, so I escaped with Maggie."

"Can you show me where they kept you?" Jett asked.

"I could, but I can already tell you won't find shit. I returned for answers, but the place was razed to the ground."

"They might have chipped you."

Luke's lips tilted. "They might have, but I learned from my mistakes. Since I didn't have an EMP machine I did the next best thing and went to a dentist. Ran myself through the x-ray machine a few times. Had to do it to Maggie, too."

"That's dangerous for the baby," Jett barked.

"So is getting caught by psychos," was Luke's retort. "What else should I have done?"

"Have you seen any sign of them since?"

Luke shook his head. "But we've been on the run, never stopping more than a day or two in any place."

"I'm going to have to tell Adrian," Jett informed him.

"I figured that."

"Why not tell him yourself?"

Luke took a moment to reply, as if the answer troubled him. "I can't go near him because I desperately want to return."

The words didn't entirely surprise Jett. He'd suspected for a while that the magnet drawing the projects back wasn't a place but a person.

One person.

Chimera.

The father of monsters had disappeared, but his children kept coming back.

CHAPTER FIVE

ADRIAN CHIMERA DIDN'T SUFFER REGRET OFTEN, but he did feel bad about setting the empty house on fire, especially since it looked just about done. The stickers from the manufacturer were still in the windows. A homeowner's dream about to become a burnt-out insurance nightmare.

You'd think, given it was the third one in as many evenings, he'd feel less remorse. But Adrian was a man who hated waste. Look at the wasted resources being reduced to ash. Almost as bad as those who wasted life.

When he saw those with no motivation, no drive, he wanted to shake them. Slap some sense into them and remind them they never knew what tomorrow might bring.

Adrian spent the first half of his life in a body that kept decaying, going from able-bodied to crippled in a wheelchair. The fact he ever managed to achieve the science necessary to repair himself was a miracle in and of itself.

The desperate gamble paid off. He was living, walking proof. But the cure wasn't quite perfect.

You're insane.

No, I'm not.

Because having conversations with the voices in his head wasn't crazy at all.

The flick of the match against the cardboard resulted in a flame. He dropped the match. He left the porch at a run, his hooded sweater hiding his features on the off chance someone watched. Explain that to the authorities.

Yes, officer, I set that house on fire, but I had a good reason. I am trying to catch a woman who likes to walk into infernos.

There was a padded cell somewhere for people like him.

The gasoline-soaked rag that he'd dropped on the porch burned merrily, the flames hungry enough to melt the vinyl siding. Smoke filled the air, although this time of night it was more a smell than a sight.

He hunkered across the street, the shadow of the excavator left behind for the next day's work a good shield from behind which to watch. The erratic dance of the flames hypnotized and made him wonder how long his old lab burned once he gave the command to destroy it. The very fact he'd made a plan to blow up his lab in the first place just went to show how far down the rabbit hole he'd fallen.

There was no climbing out. No redemption for him. Also, no damn proof he'd done anything. Between the charges that exploded and the chemicals left behind, they'd turned his life's work into a raging, melting blaze that wouldn't be easily put out by simple water. Even if someone sifting the ruins found an intact hard drive, good luck getting any information. The virus he'd run on the network wiped everything clean. He'd watched and learned from the errors of past science greats both real and fictional.

As the fire spread across the front of the house, licking up the siding, lighting the night sky, Adrian wondered if he wasted his time. For all he knew, the woman he sought was clear across town visiting another burning building. Or didn't exist at all. What if the videos were fake? She could have died in the last sighting.

This is stupid. He chased an impossible dream. A second chance he didn't deserve.

And then he saw her. Hips sashayed as she suddenly stepped out of the shadows, an undulating Venus with her rounded hips, indented waist, and handful-sized breasts tickled by hair that appeared dark but could have been the auburn he knew so well. There was a languid grace about her movements, and he couldn't help but stare at the woman. Was it Jane?

She approached from the far side where he couldn't quite see her face.

He'd have to move, which might startle her. But the important part was she'd come. Now he'd find out once and for all if it was Jane or a look-alike.

He ducked out of from behind safety of the tractor onto the road, feet pounding on the pavement to reach the sidewalk.

The woman never once turned her head, just kept walking toward the dancing flames. Their hungry orange tendrils edged closer to the roofline, spreading and growing to brighten the dark.

The woman didn't appear daunted by the inferno and kept approaching, closer than he dared. He couldn't let her get away.

"Hey. You," he shouted to no reply.

She reached for the knob of the house, which had been locked when he tried it. Yet turned in her grasp. The door swung open, and she took a step over the threshold, about to disappear inside.

No. He couldn't lose her. Desperate, he yelled, "Jane, stop."

The woman paused and then cast him a glance over her shoulder, a gaze with eyes kaleidoscope in color, freakishly bright and unnatural.

The flames all around lit her in a glow, and her hair appeared as a burning nimbus draped over her shoulders. She perused Adrian, dismissed him, and entered the house.

Adrian started after her, feeling the heat licking at his skin, sucking at all the moisture. The very air scorched his lungs. "Jane," he yelled again, because he'd lost all doubt. As impossible as it seemed, she lived.

And she might die if she didn't get out. He tried to get closer to the inferno, only an explosion rocked the house, the windows shattering outward, sending a tremble into the ground. He wavered on his feet and then covered his face and head as debris rained down. A smoldering piece of something hit the ground beside him.

Sirens approached, and he cursed. He needed a few more minutes to look for Jane.

Or not. He stared at the completely consumed wreck. Between the smoke and the fire, no one could have survived.

No one human, that was.

As with the other scenes, the firemen found no remains in the house.

No sign of her at all. But Adrian wasn't about to give up. Jane was out there, somewhere. He was sure of it.

I have to find her. Had to explain. Atone.

He did his best, only to fail night after night but not for lack of trying. Adrian ran around the city setting fires, one each night in a different locale. Three since the night he'd seen her. And not a single sighting.

It took Jett taking the lighter from his hand when

he eyed a firework outlet store before Adrian snapped out of it. "This isn't working," he muttered.

"Ya think?" was Jett's sarcastic drawl. "It's time you went home."

"But Jane..." Adrian murmured her name. Still amazed she'd recovered. Curious about how she survived the fire. And why was she drawn to them?

"Are you even sure she's alive?" Jett asked, not for the first time.

"Yes." A certainty he couldn't explain.

"Even if she is, Jane obviously doesn't want to be found."

"She's confused."

"Or pissed." Jett, the voice of stark reason.

"I need to find her."

"Ever think she doesn't want anything to do with you?"

Adrian glared. "You're not being helpful."

"Sorry, would you prefer I bowed and said yes to every stupid thing you say?"

Adrian pressed his lips into a tight line. "No. But it's Jane." Jett couldn't understand why he had to help. Why he had to find her. "She has to be somewhere."

"Yup, and I'll wager she's watching," Jett remarked, helping him to their car.

"And not showing herself?" Adrian frowned. "Why not?"

"Gee, maybe because you left her to die in that

explosion. Wouldn't be the first time one of your patients didn't appreciate your efforts."

Adrian's lips pursed. "But she wasn't awake. She has no idea I treated her."

"Even if she knew you were her doctor, she also has no idea who you are." Jett fixed him with a dark gaze as he pulled the car onto the road. "Keep in mind, the last time she saw you—"

"I was a puny glasses-wearing kid in a wheelchair." Adrian had changed a lot since then. And so had the world.

Jane had been sleeping for more than two decades. A lifetime full of invention. In her mind, she probably still felt eighteen, the age when she'd overdosed.

"Could be she has no memories at all," Jett added. "Weren't you the one saying she was a vegetable?"

Adrian scowled. "Don't say that. She was sleeping."

"Sleeping like the dead." Jett wasn't one to couch things. "And now she's not."

Probably on account of what Adrian did. "I cured her."

"Maybe. Or maybe she's the start of the zombie apocalypse."

It took him seeing the slight quirk of Jett's mouth to realize he jested.

"I have to find her."

"You ain't finding her. Not unless she wants to be found."

"So what do you suggest I do?" Adrian snapped. Of late it happened more often.

"Go home."

"What the fuck am I supposed to do there? Twiddle my fucking thumbs?" Adrian asked with some sarcasm.

"Actually, you need to start prepping. Or have you forgotten about Becky and the babies?"

"I haven't forgotten. I get the ultrasound machine this week." Adrian drummed his fingers on the car door.

"You're going to need more than that. When was the last time you delivered a baby?"

"Excuse me?"

Jett stopped at a red light and gave Adrian his attention. "An old friend of yours needs your help."

It took him only a second to grasp who Jett meant. "You've spoken to Luke?"

"Yeah."

The knowledge almost blew his mind. "When?"

"A few times since we got to town."

Adrian exploded. "And you didn't tell me?"

Rather than apologize, Jett shrugged. "I'm telling you now."

"How did you find him?"

"I didn't. He contacted me."

Mind blown again. "He's sane?"

"As sane as a guy with a super pregnant wife can be. But he's looking for help."

"Of course, I'll help. Bring him to me."

Jett shook his head. "Not so quick. Before you meet, he wants assurances."

"And he went to you to ensure them?" It burned that Luke would have approached Jett instead of Adrian. At one time, they'd been friends. But apparently, according to Luke, Adrian ruined things when he kept experimenting on Luke. Didn't his friend understand he was trying to achieve perfection?

"He came to me because I understand. My wife's also pregnant with a child who is..." Jett trailed off as the light turned green.

"Your children are the next stage of evolution."

"Or the downfall of it. I love my wife, and I'll love our kids, but let's not kid ourselves here, boss. What you've accomplished could change the face of humanity."

"About time." It wasn't as if humanity had that much to offer. Adrian might have been cured for over a decade now, but he never forgot the taunts. The depression. The feeling of rejection.

He also never forgot what revenge felt like. Jane used to be his daily reminder of what happened when vengeance wasn't tightly focused. But Jett didn't know about his dirtiest secret of all.

"Luke only wants to deal with you and me," Jett said.

"What makes him think he can trust you?"

"My wife." Jett grimaced. "Apparently, Becky has

been chatting with Margaret for a while now. She promised I would help."

Adrian knew better than to expect Jett to break that promise. "When does he want to meet?"

"Soon. He won't be giving any warning. Just expect him to show up."

"At least he didn't wait too long. She's what, five, six months along?"

Jett shook his head. "According to Luke she might be further along. Says she looks ready to pop any day."

Accelerated growth? Certainly a possibility.

"I wish he'd not waited so long to contact me," Adrian noted. "If there are complications, it might be too late to intervene."

"First off, don't use the word intervene around Luke. He's liable to rip your face off. And second, you better hope neither of them dies." Left unsaid, Luke would kill him if they did.

"You're getting on the highway," Adrian observed, recognizing their path.

"Told you, it's time you went home. Your luggage is already in the trunk."

A part of him wanted to argue. To demand his employee turn the car around. He kept quiet, because he realized Jett was right.

Time to stop chasing Jane. This torching of places wasn't working, and sooner or later, the cops would catch up.

He needed better bait.

CHAPTER SIX

She kept watch long after the noisy metal box left. Mostly because of her fascination with one of the males that climbed inside.

He drew her with his strong presence. He delighted with his ability to start lovely warm fires for her to bask in. Except, once she realized he set them for her, she stopped enjoying them. Mostly because she wondered if the fires he set were part of his mating ritual.

Did he seek to attract her?

It only partially worked. Because while the infernos delighted, the male discomfited.

He seemed familiar. The timbre of his voice. Something in the general shape of his face. But his scent... she didn't recognize it at all. Even as it intrigued her.

She was drawn to the man, which made her suspicious. Hence why she ignored his offerings and watched instead.

And then he was gone. The first night of no fires she spent searching, not for the flames but *him*.

Only he was nowhere to be found.

She did eventually find some warmth in the form of coals burning under a bridge. Standing on them gave her a sense of peace until some noisy males thought to touch her. Their screams pleased almost as much as the scent of their burning flesh.

As she chewed on some crispy fat, enjoying the quiet she created, she pondered why the interesting male had left.

Don't care. A claim she kept repeating to herself, yet she looked for him again the next night.

And then the third.

It wasn't until the fourth she realized he wasn't coming back. Had he given up?

For some reason that bothered her. Especially since she missed him and had decided she needed to know more about this strange male. Why did it feel like she should recognize him?

Why had he stopped coming?

On the fifth night, a bright flare caught her attention as a sudden inferno erupted. Thinking he'd returned, she raced across the city, only to arrive too late. Noisy metal machines with flashing lights arrived before her. The males in their bulky suits held long snakes that spewed water.

Way to ruin a perfectly good fire.

From her perch atop a roof, she watched and only barely heard the arrival of another. She whirled and beheld nothing. Yet she could have sworn she didn't stand on that roof alone.

A voice whispered. Words she could almost understand but garbled as if filtered. She shook her head and took a step toward the shadows, a darkness that shifted. A shape moved, shifted, and spoke a word that registered. "Revenge."

Her nostrils flared at the mention, and she growled.

The arm pointed, finger extended into the distance. A direction to follow. "Revenge," the voice repeated.

And she understood what she had to do.

She left the city that night in search of him.

CHAPTER SEVEN

NOT MUCH WAS SAID DURING THE LONG RIDE BACK
to Adrian's house in the woods.

As the miles whipped by and the scenery became
more desolate, the stretches of dense forest growing
longer, he had to wonder if he'd made the right choice.

He'd left Jane behind. Poor confused Jane, who,
through some miracle, woke and now had no idea what
had happened to her.

I should have done better in tracking her down.
Yet the closest he might have gotten to her was a
basement room. Decrepit with a single sink and a
mattress on the floor. But it was warm. The pile of
garbage on the floor and the oil slick in the corner
had created a nice smoldering blaze that was easily
extinguished in that concrete space once the fuel
ran out.

The police called it the work of vagrants, but

Adrian wondered if perhaps it was Jane, so he'd visited the location.

One half of the cell-like room was covered in charred marks, the soot thickly layering the surface. Yet the spot where the mattress lay was perfectly clean. Unburned. Which meant the red strands of hair left on the stained mattress were easy to spot.

Jane was here.

She just never returned. Not to that room at any rate.

But...what if she, like his other patients, felt a need to return to her maker? To find the man who'd changed them all.

He'd rather deal with her in familiar territory.

Which was why he asked Jett a few questions as they drove. "Did you extend the security system past the perimeter of the house?" Adrian worried about more than simple burglars.

"The motion detection lights and cameras have been placed to the edge of the woods."

"None within the forest?" he asked.

Jett shot him a look. "Cameras are best placed in open spaces where movement is detectable. In the woods, there are many false positives, given the small animal life and always moving foliage."

"Surely you program them to only react to large items."

"Yeah. I could. Which begs the question, why? I thought you said this place was safe."

"It is."

"Which we both know is bullshit." Jett paid attention to the road ahead of him, the middle yellow line the color in the headlights. "Someone attacked the clinic. That kind of act smacks of desperation."

"Doesn't it though." Adrian looked out the window as unrelenting darkness marched by. "But we haven't seen hide nor hair of that person since, which more than likely means they got what they wanted when they captured Dr. Cerberus."

"Or they're biding their time. Hell, maybe they're the ones who helped the transported patients escape."

"One would hope they wouldn't be so stupid." Those that could function already lived at large. It was only those who still required help that Adrian kept under lock and key.

"Doesn't matter what they were thinking. Those patients are gone. Hopefully the winter will take care of them."

"Such a lack of empathy. And to think it is my patients we call feral." The comment earned Adrian another dark stare.

"You hired me for my practical nature. A good thing one of us can act. What's wrong with you lately? You going soft?"

Hardly, given the recent blood on his hands.

"Let's just say I'm beginning to see things more clearly."

You keep telling yourself that, boyo.

They arrived at Adrian's house, the body of it dark, and almost invisible, on purpose. The remote location, in the woods, meant any kind of light, even a simple porch one, attracted things. Curiosity of hikers. Moths. Predators.

Which was why he waited for Jett to leave, watching until the taillights vanished before he lit up the place. If the room had an overhead light or a lamp on a table, Adrian turned it out. A beacon to anything in the forest.

A faint hope that a certain lady would somehow manage to follow him. Although, if she traveled on foot, it might take a while. The first patient to find Adrian had taken almost five days, and the lab he'd escaped from was much closer.

He was probably in for a wait, but Adrian didn't sit idly. He spent hours scouring the internet for signs of Jane. Any mention of fire in a two-hundred-mile radius caught his attention. Some were simple accidents: overturned candle, stove top fire. But then there were the less obvious ones.

Blazing car wreck on the highway.

Unexplained explosion in a chip truck.

A flaming basin of oil at a gas station.

Was Jane the cause?

Not knowing drove him to distraction. To deal with that anxiety, Adrian mulled over everything Jett had told him about Luke and Margaret. She was very pregnant, and Luke was worried enough that he sought out Adrian via Jett.

Which peeved Adrian off for a few reasons. One, Luke should have come to him! He was the one who could offer aid.

But the bigger reason Luke approaching Jett was a problem had to do with the doubts this instilled. Already Jett questioned the strangeness of Becky's pregnancy. Dealing with the fact his children might be *special*. Then Luke arrived, panicked, Margaret showing signs of an abnormal pregnancy and suddenly Jett feared. And how did Adrian know his stoic guard was worried? Because he actually said during the darkest stretch of their trip, "Will this pregnancy harm Becky?"

It felt wrong to lie. "Possibly."

Adrian could offer no reassurance because there was none to give. This was uncharted territory. The babies these women carried were the start of a new race. An exciting time for the evolution of mankind.

"Red is strong. If anyone can do this, it's her," Jett mumbled, seeking reassurance, and yet Adrian couldn't state with certainty that everything would be all right because he didn't know. Would the pregnancy affect the mother? Harm her? Would the child emerge humanish, or something else? Would they be intelligent, taking after their human half, or emerge no better than an animal? Would the bloodthirsty madness that plagued so many be their curse as well?

These types of questions didn't used to bother Adrian—before. Now that he felt his own grip on sanity slipping, he had time for regret. Even felt a sense of remorse for some of the things he'd done.

The things he might still have to do.

Too late to go back now, boyo. The fun's just about to begin.

To quiet the voice in his head, he spent the next few days in a flurry of activity: setting internet monitors for signs of Jane, ordering more equipment for his basement lab—including an incubator in case the baby was premature. Then he went on to more customized items: baby mitts to prevent scratching from nails that might be more like claws, baby bottles with sturdy rubber nipples, formula. If the child was born with a full set of teeth, the mother might not want to nurse.

Adrian also made sure his freezer was stocked with meat. Lots of it. Luke might have found his will and humanity to live, but it helped if you kept the more savage side of him fed. Or so Adrian discovered within himself. Nothing like a steak tartare for a nighttime snack when the urge to rip off his clothes and run into the woods hit him.

Do it. Feel the freedom. The rush. Let's eat al fresco tonight.

Alcohol probably wasn't the best course of action; however, he liked the warm buzz.

While Adrian fought to keep a grip on his sanity, Jett popped in and out with status reports. Mostly empty ones. The escaped patients had disappeared. The new lab was wiped clean as a precaution. The remaining staff sent to a European location out of harm's way.

All kinds of safety measure measures taken to protect those remaining, and the secret.

"We're still watching to see if any of the patients pop up into the public eye. Cop scanners, hospitals." Jett had it all covered, and Adrian didn't inform him that, by this point, he'd dispatched three former patients thus far. The latest one the night before.

The wings on Jacob's back had allowed him to glide in for the attack. But his hollowed bones meant he didn't have the weight behind it.

Rather than call his cleanup crew again, Adrian buried him in a pile of debris, branches and leaves he'd swept clean, and then set it on fire. The dancing flames made him think of Jane.

Sixteen more to go!

He had to wonder if Jett noticed anything on the cameras. Adrian, after all his questions about the security system on the ride home, had decided to disable the outside devices. He didn't want Jane spooked if she happened to decide to find him.

On the fifth day of his return home, the knock at his door drew his attention. The hairs on the back of his neck rose—*Stranger danger!*—and his lip pulled back in a partial snarl. He caught himself and schooled his features before striding to answer.

The sight that met him kept him speechless for a moment—and filled him with a strange joy.

"Take a picture, it will last longer," Luke snapped, as pleasant as ever. For all his gruff demeanor, the man looked good. Fit. Broad in the shoulder, his beard lush and full. His eyes a normal brown color without a hint of glow. No sign of the wolfman he could become.

By his side was a shorter figure swaddled in a cape that hid her shape, but he remembered the fair features of Margaret. Once a nurse at the clinic, she'd fallen for her patient, and together they'd fled. Adrian kept track of them for a while, until the tracker inside the escaped lovers was deactivated. It still bothered Adrian that some nameless party was aware of his research. It made the rage within bubble at the thought of someone trying to steal his life's work. Yet, oddly enough, they went after Cerberus rather than the true scientist himself. Rather insulting.

Maybe because they knew you were crazzzzzzzy.

"Come in." Adrian swept a hand, and the pair entered, followed by Jett, who appeared as dark and gloomy as ever. "Where's Becky?"

"It's a water day," Jett replied, meaning her mermaid side had taken over and demanded a full submersion. It happened more and more often of late.

By the lines of worry on Jett's face, Adrian could guess what he feared. That one day she wouldn't be able to transition back to land.

He placed his hand on the man's arm and sought to reassure. "It's probably just the pregnancy hormones." Which were snowballing in Becky. Her pregnancy was advancing at a much faster rate than Margaret, who had removed her cape to display a gorgeously round belly that jutted from her body and was much larger than a woman at her stage should be.

"How do you feel?" was the first thing Adrian asked.

"How do you think I feel?" was her retort. "I'm huge. And uncomfortable. Hungry all the damned time. My ankles are swelling, and I swear this kid is going to come out adult sized.

A faint smile touched Adrian's lips. "It just feels that way. If you'll follow me, I've got all the equipment set up in the basement."

"Said every mad scientist before cackling," Luke muttered.

Even Jett snickered.

They poked fun at Adrian, but good news, no one had tried killing him yet, which he considered a step in the right direction.

The basement might connote ominous overtones, but the space itself was bright and big. The house, built into the side of a hill, meant the back half of the lower level was above ground. A large sliding glass door opened onto the lower patio and provided natural light to the medical facility he'd created.

Luke whistled as he looked around. "You just can't help yourself, can you? One lab destroyed and already got a new one up and running."

"Not everything I did was bad," Adrian replied in defense of his actions.

That brought a snort. "Does that help you sleep at night?"

No. Only the cannabis oil he mixed with alcohol did. "I didn't realize you wanted us to have a discussion on the morality of my actions. Perhaps we should return upstairs to a more comfortable seating environment."

Luke's face tightened, and Margaret placed her hand on his arm. "Don't let him get to you." She turned her gaze on Adrian, not warm, or even friendly. "Let's do this. Show my husband that the baby I carry isn't going to pull an alien and rip its way out of my body."

"Not funny, Maggie," growled her protective mate.

"But the truth." She turned a look on her husband. "You've been terrified that this baby will hurt me since Sven and his buddies examined me."

"What happened?" Adrian asked as he washed his hands and slipped on a white coat.

A foreboding expression pulled at Luke's features as Margaret answered. "We went to see a guy. A biologist. He managed to get us into a clinic where he could use some of their equipment."

"What did you see?" Adrian asked while pointing to the bed he'd had delivered only the day before. No rails on it. No manacles. Unlike the ones he used to have at his clinic in the mountains.

"A moving blob," Luke grumbled.

Ultrasounds often appeared that way to those not trained to understand what they saw.

"It was a baby," Margaret said with clear exasperation.

"With a tail!" Luke exclaimed.

Adrian managed to keep his features from showing he was startled, but Jett didn't. "A tail? That's nothing. How about I raise you a tail and add fins. My wife's got a pair of tadpoles swimming around in her tummy."

For some reason three sets of eyes turned on Adrian, who raised his hands. "Don't start. Margaret's is the first pregnancy that's been viable past the first trimester. And as for Becky...I'll admit this is new territory for us all."

Very new, since the last few pregnancies of patients with staff resulted in miscarriages, and one of the mothers didn't survive. In his defense, no one had expected her to commit suicide after the miscarriage. But after that, they were much more careful to ensure none of the women saw the child until they'd had a chance to check it over.

"Let's stop screwing around. Get on with it," Luke growled.

Margaret lay on the bed, and Adrian grabbed the bottle of gel. She lifted her shirt to show an impressive belly, the skin stretched, the belly button popped.

A squirt of the cold gel made her tummy mountain wobble. Margaret laughed. "Junior doesn't like it."

Luke placed his hand on the moving hump, and it stilled. "Junior needs to behave for a minute while the doc checks him out."

The wand slid with ease over her belly, and immediately the sound of a heartbeat filled the air. Strong, fast, much faster than the second thud of its mother's in the background.

"Only one fetus," Adrian remarked aloud as he tapped on his keyboard and slid the wand, taking measurements, doing his best to contain his excitement. The doctor in him was giddy. There was a child in there. Viable. Alive. And...different.

There was no denying certain aspects about the baby she carried, but Adrian didn't say anything aloud. Not yet. What he did instead was manage to get a good shot of the baby's face. He tilted the screen. "This is your son."

Margaret gasped, and her eyes shone with tears; whereas Luke canted his head and squinted. "He looks like an alien."

"Luke!" Margaret exclaimed.

"Man has a point," Jett added, having gotten close enough to also watch the proceedings.

"All babies appear alien on ultrasounds." Adrian moved the wand to show them a hand. "Four fingers and a thumb on his left hand." Same for the right. "Toes." The limbs of the child's arms and legs perfectly formed. "No claws," he added to reassure.

"What about..." Luke didn't say it.

So Adrian moved the wand and said it for him. "The tail? It's still there, but I should note that, while rare, babies are still born every year with them."

"Is this your way of saying he's normal?"

"No." Adrian didn't couch the truth. "Your child is different. How could he not be given who his father is? But"—Adrian held up a hand to forestall Luke's next question—"he is healthy. The rest of him is perfectly formed, if a bit large."

"So he's not five months old?"

Adrian shook his head. "Given his size, I'd say he's full term or close to. His lungs appear perfectly formed, which is usually the concern in preterm births. My recommendation is we deliver your wife soon to avoid complications."

"What kind of complications? Is the baby too big?" she asked.

Adrian shrugged. "By my measurements, close to ten pounds, which is not in and of itself unusual. But you have narrow hips. If we wait too long, a natural birth might not be feasible."

"My mother had me via C section," she admitted. "Apparently I had a big head."

Luke snickered. "Isn't that my line?"

"Luke!" Margaret exclaimed, slapping him in the arm

The man sobered to ask, "Other than having a giant squash, can the baby hurt her?"

Adrian shrugged. "I wish I could say no with one hundred percent certainty, but with every pregnancy, there is a possibility of something going wrong."

"All things I already told you." Maggie swung her legs over the table and sat up. "When should we schedule the inducement?" she asked Adrian.

"Soon. I'll need to get some more materials first. But I don't want to delay too long."

He also made sure to get some samples from her: blood, urine. She vetoed the amniotic fluid test.

"How can I contact you?" Adrian asked as he saw them to the door.

"You don't. I'll be in touch," Luke said.

Closing the door, Adrian leaned on it and closed his eyes. Elation at the first birth of one of his patients filled him.

Success. Finally, after so much failure. But at the same time, trepidation hit him. Not just for the baby, the first natural born of his kind. What would the child be like? Would it develop like a normal human child, or would the animal characteristics take over? Was Luke right to fear?

And then there was Luke. A man who'd been on the brink of death, having given up on life. Now, he appeared saner and healthier than ever, but only because of Margaret.

Adrian didn't have a Margaret. And the madness crept closer.

Close? I'm already here, motherfucker!

CHAPTER EIGHT

A DAY HAD PASSED SINCE LUKE'S VISIT, AND Adrian occupied it spending large sums of money rushing to prepare, a sense of urgency filling him.

It felt as if he snowballed toward something. Good? Bad? He couldn't tell. But he suspected it had to do with Jane. Every time he turned a corner, he expected to see her.

Which was weird and oddly ominous, given he wasn't one to believe in portents.

Forget it, boyo. She isn't coming. Why would she come to you? He could almost see his mind, the split part of it curling its lip in disdain.

I can help her.

Sure, you can. With a bullet to the brain, just like you did to the others.

They attacked me, he justified, arguing with himself.

Can you blame them, boyo?

He'd never meant to hurt anyone. He simply wanted to heal. Why did no one appreciate that?

Give a blind man back his sight and he complained about the suckers that appeared on his body—a little too much starfish in that one. Regrow a leg that was blown off in a war, and the patient whined about the fact he could create webs.

Surely a few side effects were worth it?

Are they? the voice asked.

And to this day Adrian still said yes.

But would Jane feel the same way?

Where are you? Sitting outside on his upper deck, he stared at the flickering flames in his fire pit, not just a pretty accessory anymore. He lit it every night to stave off the cold—and in hopes of attracting a certain fiery lady.

He'd yet to catch a glimpse of Jane, not in person and not on any of his cameras, their feed temporarily rerouted to his eyes only lest Jett give him another speech on not being an idiot.

It was probably a vain thing to even imagine Jane might be drawn to him like some of his other patients.

I am the magnet and they the metal irresistibly drawn. Like Lori-ann, who launched herself with a scream through an upstairs window. Unluckily for her, he was ready. It took two bullets—the first one grazing her shoulder, the second in her gut as she landed on him—before she slumped in his arms, doing her best to bite, the drool hanging in wet threads from her prominent canines.

Given how close that was, despite his shooting skills, he talked Jett into giving him self-defense lessons the next day. Getting tossed onto his back over and over helped him not dwell on Jane's fate. He spent some of the time gasping for air through heaving lungs, or aching ribs, thinking of Luke and Margaret, soon to be parents of the first hybrid child.

And if the child lived...the start of a new era for humanity.

Adrian couldn't wait to tell the world what he'd accomplished. When he began rolling out the Chimera Treatment—named in his honor of course—he'd put an end to childhood disease and severe injury. No more drugs, no more hospitals.

Perfect health for all—if you didn't mind the tail or the teeth or the urge you had to run through the woods chasing things.

No worse than the drugs they had nowadays. He'd heard of one drug recently that had a possibility of penile necrosis. Made a tail seem like a good thing.

Adrian shifted, the evening deepening, leading him to maudlin thoughts. Wondering about Jane. It had been a week since he'd left the city. And every single day he thought about going back.

To do what? Set more fires and hope she came by? Perhaps had he brought along a bag of marshmallows for roasting it would have added some allure.

I should return. Try harder. Pull out all the stops.

He tempered his urge with the reminder that Jane was probably gone. Monitoring the news, he knew there had been few blazes of note and no sightings of the naked redheaded woman. Could be she'd moved on or that she'd died. For real this time.

Except he refused to believe it.

Shifting away from the propane fire feature with its perfect flames and slight radiating heat, he took in a deep lungful of air, the feel of it cold and crisp.

Winter crept closer. Soon he'd wake to frost in the morning. Would Jane know to find a warm place to hide?

He tossed back the last of his scotch, the heat of it no longer burning as it went down. He'd already had a few too many given the pleasant buzz.

Adrian wondered if his drunkenness was to blame for the sudden change in the scent of the fire at his back, as if cinnamon and cloves had been dumped on it. It was an intoxicating smell. He whirled to see what caused it. Had something fallen onto the flames?

He saw nothing in the fire bowl, only the shiny lava rocks providing a bed for the dancing flames. They stretched higher than before and, like fingers, stretched to grasp him.

Recoiling from the heat didn't help. The burning scent of spice increased just as a hand grabbed hold of his neck and tossed him hard enough that he hit the side of his house and fell to the deck. Before he could recover, the alcohol making his movements sluggish, he was grabbed again and rammed against a wall. He might be pinned, but his feet remained flat on the ground given the rather short stature of the woman holding him there.

Not all that intimidating in a sense, but he didn't fight back. He gaped in wonder, for wearing her long hair—and nothing else—so it dangled over her breasts was the lovely Jane.

"Hi," was his suave greeting to the naked woman on his deck.

Hers was to toss him as if he weighed nothing. He flew, sans wings, and landed with a clumsy slide that rammed him into the glass railing. Face first. Smushed like a cartoon bug.

He didn't remain there long. He scrambled to his feet and held out his hands as the woman strode to him, hips undulating, a distracting sight that no one could have resisted. But he did his best, keeping his gaze on her, noticing the glowing kaleidoscope color in her eyes.

"Jane." He tried to keep the word low and reassuring. It didn't stop her stalking. He shifted to the left in an attempt to remain out of reach. "I know you're probably mad." No probably about it. He'd left her to die in his condo. She should have died when the explosion went off or in the subsequent fire. But tell that to the pissed-off woman who kept pace with him, an aura of danger rolling off of her.

She still wore no clothes, and yet she wasn't dirty. She glowed, her skin bearing a rosy tint, and she exuded warmth in spite of the low temps outside.

His sluggish science brain started making the connections. "You woke up because of the fire in the condo." Had instinct kicked in and forced her to run from the danger?

Except that didn't feel right. He added in the other facts he knew. "You like heat." And heat liked her. The flames followed her as she moved around the fire pit, her head turned to keep an eye on him, but her fingers trailed through the hot stones. Yet she didn't recoil or flinch. Her lips parted on a happy sigh.

Impervious to heat and, in turn, craving it. How could this be? Fire was supposed to destroy. He didn't know of a single creature that wouldn't succumb. Certainly nothing he'd given her should have allowed this kind of evolutionary change.

Tell that to Jane, who leaned down and embraced the flames. He could only stare. Jaw on the ground— and oddly aroused, too.

Jane was hot. Her eyes reflected all the colors in the fire. Her lips were parted and soft, inviting. Her hair dangled in the flames and glowed like embers, piping-hot red. And her breasts...he wondered if he'd burn himself touching those red-tipped berries.

What a way to die.

He shook his head and tried to keep his gaze on something other than her body.

"You found me," he said.

She'd yet to say anything. A glance in her direction showed her not even paying him attention. She nuzzled the flames.

A little disturbing. "How did you find me?" Was she, like the others, drawn to him by some sort of scent? Yet surely any kind of odor wouldn't leave a trail that far.

She cocked her head, finally staring at him, yet he saw no sign of recognition. There was nothing cognitive in her gaze.

"Do you remember your name?" he asked, taking it as a good sign she was no longer trying to choke him. The effects of the alcohol dissipated as his brain fired with interest. It helped that the blood in his body was pumping—in the wrong direction.

She straightened from the fire and took a step toward him.

Adrian held his ground. "Your name is Jane."

Her full lips moved, but she didn't say a sound.

"I'm Adrian. Adrian Chimera. Do you remember me?"

At the query, she blinked. "Aaaaaadreeeaan." The moan-like quality of his name made him shiver. But her repeating it was a good sign. A very good sign.

"Yes. Adrian. We used to go to school together."

The blank expression remained.

"Do you want to come inside? I really should examine you." He reached for her, and she hissed.

More disturbing was the sudden glow and lift of her fiery hair.

"No touching. Very well." He tucked his hands behind his back. "If you'll just follow me." He didn't like to give her his back, but in order to lead, he'd have to show her a direction.

She didn't pounce on him, which he took as a good sign. He entered his house, the living room a vast two-story affair with grand windows overlooking the forest, but she made a beeline for the fireplace. The flames danced merrily behind the glass screen.

Smash. Her fist went right through it, and she grabbed the flame. Literally grabbed fire and then stood with it dancing on her palm. She didn't look at Adrian, rather grinned happily at the impossibility in the palm of her hand.

Did she not feel pain at all? The scent of cinnamon and cloves filled the room, and understanding hit him.

She's the one exuding the smell. Some kind of pheromone he'd wager, given his intense desire. They'd have to find a way to tamp it down. His arousal hurt.

Jane was his patient. A doctor should never be untoward. Which was funny considering when the disease started its debilitating trek through his body he would have welcomed anyone touching him. Especially some of the prettier nurses. But that only happened in movies. Truth was no one paid him any mind until he was out of the wheelchair and declared he was a doctor.

And now he was the one with ethics. Staring at the woman he'd tended for close to a decade, he had to remind himself of the fact that while he might know her intimately as her physician, he was a stranger to her. She'd been asleep while he did his best to bring her back.

"Do you remember your name?" he asked, approaching her slowly.

She played with the tiny flame, bouncing it from hand to hand then raising her arm so it slid the length of it and perched on her shoulder.

"Can I see your hand?" he asked, knowing what he'd see but still needing to be sure. He mimed holding out his hand.

She aped him, revealing a smooth palm, not a single mark or bubble.

"Utterly incredible," he breathed, and, until Jane, he would have insisted completely impossible. While Adrian had created many wonderful things, including hybrids capable of breathing under water, this manipulation of fire was not biological in nature by any stretch of the imagination. Her evolution was a miracle.

The fire flickered at her shoulder, and suddenly curious, Adrian reached out. The flame flared in alarm, the heat of it very real. Enough he drew his fingers sharply away.

She grinned, showing perfect white teeth that parted to better pop the flame into her mouth. Her lips sealed, but she didn't swallow. Probably absorbed the flames.

"You're fireproof," he stated aloud. An explanation for how she survived the fire. "The flames—or is it the heat? —feed you." His mind whirled with the sudden possibility. Had it been the fire itself that revived her? Something in the cleansing burn that woke her from her slumber? It could explain her affinity for infernos since. She needed it to fuel the change in her DNA. But how? How had this happened?

He HAD to know more. "I wish you could talk."

She canted her head and blinked.

He also wished she'd put some clothes on because her naked body was beyond distracting. While Adrian had gone a little wild when he first recovered, bedding every woman who said yes, he'd pretty much stopped once he got a hold of Jane. Somehow it seemed wrong that he enjoyed himself with another woman while the woman he'd loved and wronged lay in a coma in another room.

But he'd not minded the abstinence. Sex, while pleasurable for the moment it lasted, left him feeling oddly empty after. Not ever completely satisfied.

And once the madness hit, the urge to hurt things growing daily, he didn't dare get that intimate. What if he lost control?

What's wrong with losing control, boyo?

Another voice answered. *He doesn't like using cold water to clean up.*

I say lick the blood clean.

The cackling wasn't easy to ignore. Times like this, he wondered how Luke handled it. How had he returned from the brink? Once a feral patient, feared by his guards, Luke managed to push back the madness. Hell, the man got married. Somehow finding within him a core of gentleness. But Luke and Margaret's pairing had a little help. The manipulation of their dreams was something Adrian used to be able to do. Until the patient who helped him play with minds slipped over the edge. Literally. Into the lake Zane went, taking his ability to join minds with him.

Problem was being in the water didn't stop Zane from manipulating dreams. After the first nightmare, Adrian took to having a wave-cancelling machine by his bedside. The bad dreams stopped. But he had to wonder if Zane still lived in the lake Adrian had left behind or moved on through one of its river tributaries. The goods news was none of them led out of the Rocky Mountains.

Movement drew him back to the present and the very naked Jane, who prowled his living room, her backside just as gorgeous as the front. He averted his gaze. Maybe he should just close his eyes? Or how about dressing her? "Let me get you some clothes."

His attempted departure led to a singe of heat flashing past him and Jane blocking his way. A low growl emerged from her, and her eyes flashed dangerously.

Rather than resort to the gun tucked in the back of his pants, he held up his hands. "I'm not planning anything bad. I swear. Just getting you a shirt to cover yourself."

Jane glanced down at her body, and he could have fist pumped when he realized she must have understood him.

"Remember clothes?" he asked softly. "You wear them on your body."

"Hhhhiiide," she said slowly.

He fought not to beam as she showed signs of cognizance. "Yes, it hides certain attributes. Keeps you warm as well. Surely you're cold." Then again, maybe not. When she'd dashed past him, he'd felt the heat rolling off her skin.

"Ko. Ko. Cold." She frowned as she struggled to speak.

"Let's get you a nice robe. I have one in my bathroom. Hanging on the door." A plush thing that would swamp her and cover everything a good doctor shouldn't look at.

Good. Ha. Been a while since I've been able to say that.

She stepped aside, which he took as assent. He led the way to his bedroom, deliberately keeping his gaze from the rumpled bed. He quickly grabbed the robe and held it out to Jane. She looked at it. Then him.

He sighed as he spread it open and held it aloft for her to step into, sliding her arms into the sleeves, snuggling into the plushness of it. When she turned, the front of it gaping, he reached for the sash.

He ignored her hiss of warning and tied it securely around her waist. Temptation out of sight, just not out of mind.

He stepped back. "That's better." For him at least.

She frowned down at the robe. "Hide."

"Yes. And not burning, I see, which is good." He'd wondered if the heat she harbored might react to the flammable product.

Since the bed in the background proved a bit distracting, he wandered out of the room, not looking back to see if she followed but assuming she did. While he was tempted to draw her down to the lower level where he might convince her to let him do a few tests, he had a feeling that might be pushing things too far too fast.

Rather, he wandered into the kitchen and opened the fridge, drawing a yowl from her.

He turned to see her glaring at the fridge. Or was it the cold? He drew out a covered dish and closed the fridge.

She lost a bit of her scowl. He yanked the fridge open again. She sprang back, her mouth wide on a yowl of discomfort.

The cold set her off. Good to know.

She remained on the other side of the kitchen island as he bent down and stuck the meal in the microwave. While it cooked, he talked.

"How much do you remember? Do you know your name?" He repeated some of his questions from earlier. Mostly because now she seemed calm enough to listen.

Her lips pursed.

"You are Jane." He pointed at her. "I am Adrian." He jabbed his chest.

"Adrian." The word emerged slowly but understandable.

"Yes, Adrian. We used to go to school together."

Her brow wrinkled.

"I'm a doctor now."

That earned him a blink from incredibly long and thick lashes.

"Do you know what a doctor is? We examine people. Make sure they're okay," he explained to her continued blank look.

The microwave beeped, and she startled, the scent of burning spices filling the air. A reaction to certain stimuli.

"It's just the food. Hold on." He needed a dishcloth to pull out the piping-hot dish. He placed it on the counter and peeled off the lid, releasing an aromatic steam. "Leftover lasagna. Let me grab a fork."

He turned to grab one from a drawer. When he turned around, it was to find Jane stuffing the pasta into her mouth. "Or not." He let the fork clatter onto the island and watched her.

She was obviously hungry, which made him

wonder how she'd been feeding herself since the condo explosion. She didn't show signs of emaciation.

"You thirsty?" He eyed the fridge then ignored it in favor making her a cup of coffee.

He set the mug in front of her, and she eyed it, leaning down to sniff. Wrinkled her nose but still brought it to her mouth for a sip. Spat it right back out and glared at him.

"Hold on. I think I can fix that for you." He brought out the sugar bowl and dumped a spoon in. She arched a brow. He dumped in two more. Only after the fourth did she bring the cup to her lips again and take a sip. Then made a noise of pleasure as she guzzled it down, slapped it on the counter, and eyed him.

"More?"

"Mawrr," she exclaimed.

It took two more cups of coffee and loads more sugar before she wandered from the kitchen back to the living room. She paused by the couch before sitting on it gingerly. "Sew. Fa," she enunciated slowly.

"That's right." He stayed just far enough out of reach she didn't tense up. Something he'd noticed she did if he strayed too close.

"Do you know what this is?" He nudged the coffee table.

She glanced at the glass surface and grinned. "Der. Tea."

A rueful grin pulled his lips. "Yes, it's dirty. I've

been remiss in hiring someone to clean the house. Too busy working."

At her inquisitive gaze, he thought it was time to show her. "I'm a doctor. Would you like to see?" Rather than reply, she stood, and he led the way down the stairs to his lab. He had stepped fully into it before he realized she hadn't completely followed. She stood on the bottom step, eyes glowing again, her body trembling.

"Hos. Pee. Tull."

So she did remember something. In this case, probably the sound of the machines as they hummed, doing their best to keep her alive.

He circled around the bed. "I'm a doctor. I fix people. I fixed you. You were in a coma from a drug overdose." Such a tragedy to happen to someone so young and on prom night.

She stepped into the room and prowled the edges, the smell of burnt cloves and cinnamon overpowering. The lab was putting her on edge.

"Nothing to be scared of, Jane. You're all better now."

"Bett. Rrrr." She glanced at him. "You."

"Yes, me. I healed you." He couldn't help but brag as he neared her. "You were pretty much dead. The doctors had given up hope. They were going to let you die. But I saved you. I gave you a treatment that brought you back to life." He reached out to grab her hand, feeling the heat of it, the shock of awareness.

For a moment, she said nothing, just froze, her gaze locked on him. The air between them felt charged with something. It raised every hair on his body, and Jane sucked in a ragged breath.

Followed by a long, drawn-out scream. "What-didyoudo!"

CHAPTER NINE

THE FLASH OF AWARENESS HIT HER LIKE A lightning bolt. She remembered everything. Every. Friggin'. Moment.

Paralyzed in that hospital bed. Hooked to machines. Being forced to stay alive. An out-of-body prisoner, tethered to her fleshly remains, unable to die.

The horror of it was too much. Her mind snapped back to the blankness.

Screamed, *Danger!*

Where? Her gaze narrowed. It had to be the male of the intriguing scent who thought he could hold her. She snatched her hand from him and ran for the view of the outdoors that she could see. Except there was something in her way. She bounced off an invisible surface and let out a scream of rage. Her fist drew back and punched forward.

Tinkle. She smashed through the glass, the shards

hitting the ground, slicing her flesh as she pushed through the hole she made. But she didn't care.

The need to flee pulsed inside her, sending her vaulting over the rail. She hit the ground hard in a crouch.

She ran into the woods, the shadows and foliage welcoming her to hide in its depths. In the distance, she heard the male shouting.

"Jane. Come back. Dammit. Jane!"

The words made sense and didn't. She refused to acknowledge them, as a primal need to survive became her only focus. Soon she was deep in the woods.

Far enough that she slowed. A bad idea. Without the adrenaline coursing, she felt the cold. It seeped all around her, seeking to smother her and drive her back down into a deep sleep.

No.

She couldn't allow that to happen. Having just fed on some flames, it wasn't hard to pull them forth. She pressed her palm against the leaves moldering on the ground, and they ignited with a whoosh. Only a moment of true warmth.

She needed better fuel. Scouting around, she found a stump, its tree having long fallen and now a moss-covered sentinel. But the base had been left behind. Its hollow bowl gave her a spot to dump in more leaves. Branches, too. She ignited the new pile, the fire contained by the moist trunk. She'd learned her lesson after the first night she spent in the wild.

A fire too big didn't always obey her command. It raced out of control, which brought the nasty water bombers. They hummed in the sky with their huge wings before dropping the stuff. Smothered her in its clinging powdery embrace. It brought a scream to her lips as it sought to steal her inner flame.

A good thing there was a stream nearby to cleanse her.

She learned afterwards, much like in the city, to keep her fires contained. The trunk smoldered pleasantly, the fire taking root and creating heated embers for her to perch on. She tucked her arms close, barely noticing the loss of the thing the male had placed over her body.

The softness of it had pleased, as did his scent. Probably better it was gone lest it confuse her.

He muddled her brain, made her remember things.

The place she used to live. It flashed in her head. The pinkness of its walls. The mottled colors of the fabric covering where she slept. Things all around, familiar and alien at once.

My room.

She no sooner thought it than it changed to that of her prison. The ceiling high overhead but not high enough. Where was the open sky? Why couldn't she move?

She never moved. Couldn't. And she didn't truly see. More as if she sensed things around her. Sometimes she felt the vibration of sound, a strange rumble she could at times understand. Other moments, she clung to the change in temperature, enjoying the slight increase in warmth, too few and far between. Once she even managed to flutter her lashes and part her lips. The heat doing its best to drive the cold out.

There was noise as she almost stirred. A voice, angry and yelling. "I need someone to fix the air conditioner today!"

Who was that yelling?

Someone who watched over and kept her locked in that cold cell. Surely, they were at fault for her condition.

"I'm so sorry, Jane." For some reason she kept hearing that repeated over and over, especially since meeting the male of the intriguing scent. His was the voice.

Sorry for what?

For keeping me prisoner!

She stirred on her nest of glowing coals, soaking in the heat, rustling in agitation.

Should have killed him. Yet she'd stopped. The food helped. He'd given her something other than flames to eat. She'd stuffed it in her face, unable to stop herself as she finally tasted something other than ashes.

Although the meat under the bridge was tasty.

But a part of her rebelled against doing that again. A tiny voice said, *We don't eat humans.*

Why ever not? They tasted quite delicious.

Despite that fact, she went after other prey. The

kind that used four legs to run. The critter with the long ears also crunched nicely when roasted. Even the wet fish she pulled from the water sated another hunger.

The one hunger that she didn't grasp was the pulsing one between her legs. *He'd* done it. His smell. His presence. His very maleness attracting her. A male perhaps fit enough to mate.

A quiver struck at the very thought. But that would involve returning to see him. A part of her said he was dangerous. Stay away.

But much like the moths that came to burn on her bed of flame, she just couldn't help herself.

CHAPTER TEN

"Come on, Jane. I know you're out there," Adrian muttered as he paced inside. He'd lit the fire pit, giving her a fiery beacon to follow. Inside the house he'd lit candles everywhere. They flickered from glass votives on the mantel, across the counter, in a ring on the table, even a few strewn by the large sliding door leading onto the backyard, which he'd left wide open.

After the incident a few nights night before, he'd made some changes around the place. He didn't want Jane to get hurt again.

If I'd not freaked her out, she wouldn't have run. But no. He'd panicked her enough she preferred to smash through a glass window and take off running into the dark forest at night rather than sleep in a warm bed.

Given how much predator he balanced inside, instinct told him not to chase after her. She didn't want to be found at the moment. Then there was a fact that a man being hunted by the patients he'd helped shouldn't be out alone at night. One at a time he could handle. He'd rather not try and prevail against two or more.

So that night, he'd watched her turn tail and run. He'd kept watching until the morning sun rose in the sky. Wondering if she perched on a rock, basking in the warming rays.

She's not a lizard, you bloody idiot.

For once the rebuke appeared to be his own and not one of the other voices. It reminded him to look at her not only as an interesting experiment or a marvel of science but as a person.

She is a real, living person. With curves and a scent that could not be forgotten.

He wanted her to come back and had faith in the fact that, since she'd found him once, she'd come find him again. In the meantime, he prepared, ensuring the propane tank, which ran the fireplace, was full. Had more cords of wood delivered. Ordered thick blankets and more, the delivery guy grumbling each time he showed up with another load. As for groceries, Adrian had those delivered by Jett who—upon seeing his preparations—almost insisted on staying.

The big man looked around with that flat stare of his, lingering on the box of candles Adrian had bought. Right beside the duct tape and rope. "I see you're prepping for date night."

"I don't know what you're talking about."

Jett arched a brow and hooked his thumbs in the loops of his snug jeans. "You are baiting a trap for Little Miss Firestarter. Going to tie her to a bed and tell her it's for her own good?"

A heated flush, mostly because that had crossed his mind, made him bluster. "I'm trying to help her. She's in more danger the longer she stays out there." Adrian pointed in the general direction of the big bad world.

That caused a snort from his right-hand man. "What a load of shit. Next you're going to tell me putting your dick in her pie is gonna cure her?"

"Cured Becky," Adrian muttered.

At the mention, Jett smirked. "Yeah, but I highly doubt you've got equipment as good as mine." The standard male boast.

Adrian didn't reply. That was the one part of him that didn't require fixing. But he wouldn't be using it on Jane. "She's my patient."

"Meaning?" Jett asked, taking a swig from the water bottle he'd grabbed from the fridge.

Adrian stiffened. "Meaning, a doctor should never conduct himself in a sexual manner with a patient."

Jett began to choke, coughing and sputtering, spewing water before exclaiming, "You'll experiment on the desperate, locking them in cages, even kill a few for science, but you draw the line at screwing a patient. Are you fucking kidding me?"

There was a certain irony perhaps given Adrian

might have crossed a few—possibly too many—lines, but a man had to have at least one moral of value he could stand on. "Think what you like. This was never about sex. I just want to help her." Had to because he was partially the reason why she was in a coma in the first place.

Uttering a noise, Jett shook his head. "Sad part is I kind of believe you. You are one weird motherfucker. So the plan is to capture Little Miss Firestarter. I'll call Becky and let her know I am spending the night."

Cramping his style and getting in the way. "Don't bother, you're not staying," Adrian stated. "I don't need your help handling Jane."

"You might have been taking lessons from me about sparring, but that don't make you a good fighter." Jett didn't pull any punches when it came to Adrian's skill.

"If everything goes well, then this won't come down to a fight."

Jett rolled his eyes. "You can be such a fucking moron. Of course, there's gonna be violence, which is why I should stay."

"And I said no. I told you I'm handling this myself." A stubborn insistence Adrian wouldn't back down on, and Jett finally left.

Now it's just me.

And me.

And me.

He ignored the extra presences. Each of them pushing and pulsing for dominance

Sometimes he wondered what it would be like to accept those other voices inside. Jayda claimed it was a balance of giving that inner presence what it wanted, to relieve the pressure.

In her case, killing proved cathartic. But Adrian had killed. It did nothing to ease the pulsing beasts inside.

What's the worst that can happen? Blood washed out. He didn't have nightmares. Think of how liberating it would be to run wild.

He closed his eyes against the strong push. And pushed back.

Not now. Not ever. This is my body.

For now, boyo...

Far from reassuring, especially since Adrian wasn't sure what would happen if he ever lost control. Could be he'd never regain his body again.

Like hell. He'd not fought this hard to get to this point to let anything, even his own creation, take the glory.

Shoving his doubts—making him still very human —down deep, he paced by the open sliding door, feeling the kiss of outdoor air on his skin. He'd chosen to wear all black, the athletic pants made of some flame-retardant material, as was his T-shirt. The fire extinguishers were stashed all around the house, having arrived on a pallet just that morning. Jett grumbled the entire time they unpacked them.

When ten o'clock came and went without her appearing, Adrian stepped outside, sucking in a deep breath through his nose. Pine trees and a hint of winter. Nothing else. The wind must have shifted, because he no longer smelled the smoke with a hint of spice from the forest.

But he didn't need a scent to know Jane was close.

He set the bag of marshmallows on the tiny table beside the chair with its poufy, flowered outdoor cushion. Adrian grabbed the long metal pole he'd left leaning against the chair before sitting. He threaded a marshmallow on a metal tine, his actions entirely visible through the glass rail, wondering if she watched.

Extending the pole meant the marshmallow dangled over the dancing flames, a slow roast that crisped the outer skin and melted the insides. He slid it off the end and quickly popped it into his mouth, the heat quickly forgotten because of the melting sweet taste.

"Fuck that's good." How long since he'd taken a moment to savor something simple? Too long. His entire life was about science and work and...not much else.

I cured myself so I could have no life. The stark truth was a bit too much to handle sober. Adrian put down his stick and went back into the house to grab a drink. When he returned, he tried not to react as he saw Jane held a bunch of marshmallows over the fire. He noted the lack of a stick or any other kind of tool. She'd poked her fingers into each of them.

He debated getting another beer, but instead of giving Jane alcohol, he set his bottle down on the floor before stepping out.

"Hey, Jane."

She pretended to not notice him.

"Nice night for a marshmallow roast." Casually spoken as he hit the chair, grabbed his pole, and threaded a new marshmallow on his stick. He held it out so that it bobbed alongside her fingers.

Jane grew impatient and plunged her hand into the fire, letting the sugar ignite before bringing the burning fireballs to her mouth. She ate them one by one then licked her fingers.

Staring at her lithe tongue gathering all the sugar in a moist lick was possibly more decadent than a peek at her nude body. Someone had lost her clothes again.

She reached for more marshmallows, and he smiled. "Help yourself. I have another bag in the kitchen."

"Is. Morrre," she slurred then frowned.

"Yes, plenty more."

She shook her head. "S'mores," she muttered with a flutter of her lashes and a sly smirk.

The implication startled him, but he recovered quickly. "If I'd have known you were coming, I'd have bought graham crackers and chocolate."

"Mmmm." She hummed in appreciation as she ate her second batch of burnt sugar then stretched to her full height before planting herself square in front of him. This had the disconcerting effect of putting his face level with the bottom of her breasts. If he sat in an Adirondack with its low base, he'd have been even more distracted.

He swallowed hard and craned to look at her face. "I'm glad you came back, Jane."

Her lips hinted at a smile. Jane crouched, her hands braced on the armrests of his chair, bringing her face level with his. "Happy."

"You're happy you came back, too?" It warmed his heart, especially as her smile widened further.

"Happy. Kill. Adrian." No mistaking what she said.

His ego deflated a bit. "Killing me would not be in your best interest. You need me."

Her head shook, sending those red tresses whipping. "No."

"Yes, you do." He shoved out of his seat, standing to not feel disadvantaged. She remained close, the heat of her licking at his skin. It made it hard to think, but he still managed to say, "You've been lucky so far, but winter is coming."

"Cold." She shivered.

"Very cold. You need shelter. Clothes."

"Find."

"Find how?" he retorted. "You're a naked woman with rudimentary communication skills at the moment.

You start wandering places where there are people and you'll be noticed. There are bad people out there who would hurt you."

"You." Her lip curled, the disdain clear.

Probably deserved. But the first rule of being a mad scientist?

Deny. Deny. Deny.

"I'm not your enemy, Jane. I would never hurt you." Not intentionally at any rate.

"Bad." She jabbed a finger in his chest. One syllable that conveyed a whole lot of anger.

"Don't be pissed at me. I'm the one who fixed you when you were broken." He wondered if she had the capacity to understand what he said, or was she ruled by primal impulse as her next word indicated?

"Kill."

He sighed. "Yes, you could kill me. Quite easily I'm sure. But if you do, then who will help you?"

"No need." Her face twisted as she managed to spit out the phrase.

"Don't be stubborn. I can help you, Jane."

"How?" An actual query. He could have shouted with joy.

"By helping you to regain your senses, I hope. By toning down your attraction to fire so you don't draw attention. Stay with me, and we'll find a way for you to rejoin the world."

She recoiled. "Prison."

He shook his head. "I won't lock you up." Did she sense the lie?

For a moment, she gazed at him, intent, her eyes a maelstrom of color. Hypnotic almost in their effect. Then she moved past him, an enigmatic expression on her face as she walked into his house.

He ate one last marshmallow before following.

Inside, she prowled the space, dancing her fingers over the flickering candles on the mantel. Stepping into the kitchen, she grabbed an apple from the bowl of fruit and bit into it, looking so very much in that moment like Eve in the garden with the forbidden fruit. No wonder Adam forsook his place in Eden to join her.

I'd do the same.

Utter foolishness. He didn't believe in religion. The only thing forbidden in this room was Jane herself. He would just have to turn a blind eye to her charms, remind himself that he was her doctor.

"Where have you been staying?" he asked.

Rather than speak, she pointed out the door.

"You camped in the woods? Or did you find a house?"

Crunch. Crunch. Rather than give a reply, she steadily demolished the apple while perched on a kitchen stool.

Should have offered my face.

It wasn't just Adrian who wanted to smack that voice. A few others inside thought it rude, too.

"I see you lost the robe." Might as well address the naked nymph in the room.

Her lips curved. "Burnt." She didn't specify whether intentionally by fire or if her skin itself consumed it.

Could she actually exude enough heat to burn something? Would she incinerate a lover in the throes of passion?

It wasn't compassion for a possible poor victim that kept him from planning to find out. There was something repugnant about the idea of Jane with another man. It bothered him when he was a teen and she dated Benedict. And it agitated him to contemplate it now.

"Would you like something else to wear?"

He knew she understood him by the way she glanced down at her lower body primly perched with pinned knees, the soles of her feet hooked over the bar on the stool. She sat straight and lifted a leg, crossing it over the other. A blatantly sexual move that had her arching a brow as if saying, *your turn.*

She subtly propositioned him, but he didn't react. Mostly because the doctor in him grasped there could be a variety of reasons for her actions.

One, she actually desired him. The thing he doubted the most. Adrian might be a decent-looking guy, but this was Jane. He must look old to her. A man almost in his forties, fit, though, passing for much younger. But still... It seemed too improbable that she'd want him. She was drop-dead gorgeous, a woman in her prime who could have any man she wanted.

I'll never be that man. And not just because of doctor/patient ethics. A psychiatrist might claim he conflated his feelings of rejection from when he was crippled.

He'd tell them to fuck themselves. Mostly because they'd be right. He knew he didn't deserve Jane.

She's too good for me.

Damned right she is. Which is why no one else can have her, either.

A dichotomy in his mind that he might never be able to resolve.

Anyhow, she wasn't trying to seduce him, which left what other option for her blatant flirting?

Perhaps she did it unconsciously. Sensuality in some was just as natural as breathing. She might not understand the power she had over men.

Over me.

Or she did know exactly what she did and hoped to use her wiles to soften him up. Relax him that she might get close enough to kill. Was her next step to wrap herself around him, enveloping him in the heat of her presence?

What a way to die.

No dying. Not today. He turned from her.

"I bought you some clothes." He headed for the bags sitting by the couch. Several of them. He'd had

Jett take Becky shopping, unsure what Jane would find most comfortable.

He held out the offerings, and a tiny frown creased Jane's brow.

A long finger extended. "Mine?" No mistaking the questioning lilt.

"Yes, yours. I was hoping you'd come back and got you some clothes."

He took a step forward and dropped the bags a few feet from her. "Check it out. See if you like anything."

He retreated, parking his ass on edge of the couch, watching.

It took Jane a second before she slid off the stool and went to the heap. She crouched and rustled around inside a paper bag. She pulled out a dress. Not much of one, though, he should add. According to the name, it belonged in some trendy young store. Keyword being young. The party dress got balled up and tossed with a disdainful sound.

"Not your style I take it." Which he'd known. Or assumed since he'd never seen her in anything like it.

The next bag held blouses and a skirt, also tossed aside. Then there were jeans and a T-shirt. Those got fingered and kept by her feet. The last bag had another robe. Just like the one she'd burnt but in pink.

On it went. This time she remembered to tie up the sash. She snuggled into the thick collar and heaved a happy sigh.

"You forgot the slippers," he said and indicated with his head the bag with a lump still inside.

She met his gaze for a brief moment before diving on it. She emerged with flamingo-head slippers, the pink matching her robe. She held them aloft and stared before a wide smile stretched her lips. On went the slippers and she beamed at him. "Pink."

"Your favorite color. I know." He knew everything that was humanly possible to know about her. Favorite shows. Color. Food. Like Red Delicious apples.

"Hungry." She rubbed her belly and eyed him expectantly.

"I'm not much of a chef, but I'm a hell of a re-heater," he declared as he moved toward the kitchen. She didn't scatter but perched once more on a stool. He kept talking, something that felt easy and natural given how often he used to talk to her while she was in her coma. "I did a bit of shopping because I wasn't sure what you'd be in the mood for." He opened a cupboard and swept a hand. "I've got canned noodles with tomato sauce. Chili. Some beef stews. Creamy soups. Macaroni and cheese." The kind that came in a blue box and was a staple in so many homes.

Her hands clapped together.

"Want some hotdogs with it, too?" The question was casual, but he watched her to see if she understood.

"Yesss." She hissed the word quite happily. "K. Chup." The word struggled past her lips.

He understood and then pretended to be horrified. "Ketchup on macaroni and cheese deluxe? What is wrong with you? Everyone knows you only use it on burgers, fries, and Shepherd's pie."

She squealed, and as they jested, him doing most of the jokes, she responded, either by laughter or simple syllable words. Her interaction growing by bounds.

Soon he was sliding a plate across to her heaped high with orange-colored pasta and boiled chunks of sausage on the side.

Some things hadn't changed, such as her love for this simple dish. He paired it with a glass of chocolate milk, which she guzzled with a happy hum.

Then asked for, "More."

He knew she was done when she pushed the plate away and declared, "Happy tummy."

Her third glass of chocolate milk was half-full still. But it didn't matter.

The drugs he'd given her took effect, her eyelids getting heavy, and she began to sway. Her lips pursed.

"Whatdidyoudo?" The words slurred together.

"I'm helping you."

"No." She stood and staggered from the stool. "Bad." Her knees crumpled.

When she fell, he was there to catch her.

CHAPTER ELEVEN

Fluttering her lashes, the first thing Jane noticed was the ceiling over her. Given she'd been sleeping outside since her rebirth, she understandably panicked to find herself inside and, horror of all horrors, in a bed.

I'm a prisoner again!

With an exclamation, she burst out of the sheets, and her feet hit the floor. By the time she realized she could move, she was running, heading straight for the window, the same one she'd crashed through once before. Jane held up her arms braced over her face, readying for impact.

Boing. She bounced off the surface. Stunned at the development, she didn't stop to think. She punched the thing in her way, hurting her knuckles, which, in turn, had her yelling and pounding at the glass.

"Jane!" His voice cut through her panting agitation. "Calm down."

Rather, she swung harder, and the glass vibrated in the frame. It just wouldn't break. "Aaaaah!" she wailed, verbally expressing her frustration.

Which didn't do a thing to help her.

"Stop it before you hurt yourself." Again, with his firm tone. "No matter how many times you hit it, the glass won't shatter. After the incident, I had it replaced with something hybrid proof."

She understood what he said and, at the same time, didn't. Panic fluttered in her as she found herself trapped. She flipped to face him and noted he stood a few paces away, hands outstretched. Doing his best to appear benign.

Failing.

Her eyes narrowed. He'd done this to her. Trapped her!

"Arrrrrgh." She lunged at him, but he sidestepped, narrowly missing her outstretched fingers.

"Behave yourself, Jane. This is not how a lady acts."

The remark enraged her. "Bad man," she yelled. Because she never would have fallen asleep in front of him. He'd done something to her. Put her to sleep. Imprisoned her inside. Betrayed her fragile trust.

She stalked him, the heat rising from her skin and smoking from her fingertips. She wore a thin shift that went to her ankles rather than the fluffy robe she last recalled while her feet were encased in socks rather than those pink bird slippers.

"Jesus. You're smoking." He breathed the claim in wonder and then talked fast as she neared. "Jane, you need to calm down."

Why?

She didn't want to be calm. She wanted to understand why the world seemed so familiar and difficult at the same time. Needed to understand why she hated him, knew he was to blame, and yet was drawn to him.

She reached for him with molten fingertips, but he evaded her once more. Faster than he should have been able to.

"Jane, you need to stop and listen. "

The firm command only served to heat her rage, and she ignited.

"Holy fucking shit. You're on fire!"

Not for long, she couldn't sustain the flames without a heat source. But she held it long enough that the gown she wore drifted to the floor as ash.

He gaped, and during his moment of inattention, she drove herself into him, her momentum slamming them into the wall. She pressed into him, snarling in his face, getting the full effect of his scent. His solidness. His lack of fear.

He didn't fear. The very idea stilled her.

He kept talking. "I know you're scared."

"Not scared." The reply emerged, rusty but understandable.

"It's okay to be afraid. I'd be afraid, too, if I woke in a strange place and didn't understand what was happening."

The very fact he'd pinpointed part of her angst tempered her inner heat. It didn't loosen her grip on his shirt, though, especially as she recalled why she woke in a bed. "Bad man."

"I won't deny it. There are plenty of people who would agree with you. But just so you know, I'm sorry I put you to sleep."

The easy admission caused her to blink. "Drugged me?"

"Yes."

"Kill you." She really should. She leaned in close, staring at him.

Still no hint of fear. But his scent did change. Turned into something hungry, which, in turn, kindled something within her.

"I should have asked instead of lacing your cocoa with the sleeping agent."

"Why?"

"Because I knew you wouldn't let me test you."

The claim caused a brief flash of sensations of sharp things being inserted into skin. Pinching as they took blood and tissue samples without permission. "No test."

"Why not?" he asked. "You didn't come to any harm. On the contrary, I think a proper rest in a warm place has actually helped you."

Helped? Her brow knit as she finally took stock of herself. Despite the fact she'd incinerated the gown, she remained warm. Had been warm since she woke, actually. Her body didn't ache. Her skin didn't feel dry. She glanced at the hands gripping him by the shirt. Soft hands lightly scented with an oily substance.

He'd touched her! "What do?" she growled.

"Nothing, so calm down. The lotion wasn't me. I had Becky, a certified nurse I might add, come over and give me a hand with you. She's the one who bathed you then slathered you with lotion. She left the bottle behind." He inclined his head, and she almost turned to look.

Ha. As if she'd trust him. Her gaze narrowed.

"No one hurt or molested you. I swear. All I did was take some blood and tissue samples to get a handle on what's happening to you."

"I dreaming." She knew enough about what was real to comprehend none of this could be happening.

He appeared startled she knew the truth. "You think this is but a dream?"

She shrugged. "Not real. Look." She held up a finger, and it lit like a candle. Even with muddled thoughts, she understood people couldn't do that.

He frowned and didn't reply immediately. She walked past him and exclaimed as she caught sight of her robe hanging on the wall and her slippers under it. She snuggled into them and then headed for the stairs.

"Jane, where are you going?"

He didn't demand she stay. A good thing, because she might have laughed.

Heading up the stairs, she didn't need to look to know he followed. Blame it on the strange awareness of him that she had. Almost as if they were connected.

Upstairs, she headed for the cold box—the refrigerator—which oozed frigid air when opened. She ignored the nasty temperature to eye what was inside. Better stuff than in the metal cans and cardboard boxes he'd offered before.

Seeing a loaf of bread, she grabbed it, along with an unopened package of meat and a yellow bottle. She threw the stuff on the counter, working by rote, intrigued as her hands appeared to understand what she wanted, handling the bread, slathering the mustard, and stacking it with ham. She eyed the two halves with their layers and pursed her lips.

He provided the answer. "The cheese is in the fridge in the drawer on the left."

Before he'd even stopped talking, she'd flipped around and got the chunk of white wrapped in plastic. He handed her a knife before she could tear into the package.

A moment later, with a thick slice of cheese in place, the sandwich was made and meeting her lips.

As she chewed, he talked. Again. The man never shut up.

"This isn't a dream, Jane."

"Yes, it is," she mumbled between bites. Her

certainty only increased the longer she thought about it. How else to explain how she stood in the strange kitchen of some kind of giant cabin in the woods, the log beam walls not something she'd ever seen, even on vacation. The kitchen with its granite was really nice though, as was the two-story bank of windows.

But it wasn't the location that was oddest of all, but the man facing her.

Man, and not a boy, yet the Adrian Chimera she remembered was a hunched teen in a wheelchair with bottle-thick glasses and hands that had a tendency to twitch.

"What makes you think this is a dream? Can you taste the sandwich you made?"

The tart mustard and the salty ham? "Yup." She took another bite.

"You feel emotions. Sensation. Way more than any hallucination."

"Fire." One word to stop all his arguing. People didn't make fire with their fingers.

"You're special, Jane. You've been through a lot. Is it any wonder you were reborn with a few unusual attributes? Think of yourself as Spiderman."

She snorted, momentarily amused by the image of the man in the red suit swinging on a thread. She poked herself. "Wonder Woman."

For some reason that made him smile. "Indeed, you are. I, on the other hand, am not a superhero, unfortunately. Do you remember me? Adrian Chimera."

"Not Adrian," she stated. He couldn't be because this guy was old. Perhaps it was his dad?

"I assure you, Jane, it's me."

"Old."

He stiffened. "Older than you might recall, but in excellent shape."

She eyed him. Yes, he was.

He spread his hands. "Listen, this might be a little weird, but I can explain. You've been in a coma."

"Yup, nightmare." She nodded, finished her sandwich, and immediately made another.

"No, that's just it. This is real. You finally woke up after twenty-some years—"

At his claim, she laughed. Twenty years? That was a long time. No one slept that long except for– "Rip Van Winkle."

"Excuse me? What?" He blinked at her, his expression so like his son Adrian, and yet at the same time, he was nothing like that boy. This man was virile. Strong. Capable.

"Rip Van Winkle. He slept."

For some reason her reply made him smile. "He did. Just as long as you, too. Twenty years."

"Still sleeping." Having the longest dream of her life. But obviously getting close to waking given how clear her thoughts were getting. No more of that weird dream state where nothing made sense. No more screaming without a sound coming out. She'd screamed a lot during her long sleep.

"Oh, Jane." He shook his head, his expression sad. "This isn't a dream. All of what you've seen and experienced is real. You really were in a coma."

She frowned. "Accident?"

"Of a sort. Do you remember taking the drugs after prom?"

"I don't—" She began to say she didn't do that kind of stuff, instantly indignant, only to see herself with a boy. Benedict. The bottle he pulled from a coat pocket. The tiny white pills in the palm of her hand.

Just this once. Her last coherent thought.

"You overdosed, Jane." His soft words matched the memories. "The doctors pumped your stomach. Gave you all kinds of counter drugs, charcoal, and the works. They couldn't save you. Your parents had you living hooked up to machines."

Beep. Beep. Beep. The sound haunted her, and Jane slammed her hands on her ears to shut it out. "No." It didn't happen. Couldn't have.

But he kept insisting. "I can show you. I have proof. Pictures."

"No." She shoved at his chest. "No. No. No." She denied even as she remembered that horrible feeling of being trapped. Sightless. Soundless. Senseless. Going slowly mad, listening to music for the first half of her imprisonment, her mother visiting daily, bringing sound and life with her. *Yet Mommy never heard me screaming for help.* Daddy didn't hear her either. And then, one day, they stopped coming.

"I'm sorry. Jane. So very, very sorry." There was true apology in his words.

"Shut up. You're lying." The words welled up from her, demanding his silence.

He just wouldn't stop. "I know this is hard, Jane. But you can overcome this. Look at you. You're awake. Talking."

"Shut up." She closed her eyes and put her hands to her ears, trying to block him out. Trying to not dwell on the fact she'd lost twenty years of her life. "Not real. Not happening."

"Don't put your head in the sand. You have to face reality."

"No, I don't." If she ignored him, then she'd wake up and go back to being that girl who was about to graduate and start her life.

As if he read her mind, he said, "You can't go back. You're thirty-nine years old, Jane. Not that you look it."

Thirty-nine? The very idea boggled.

"You look amazing. Let me show you." He moved out of reach. A good thing since she was tempted to throttle him. Anything to stop the flow of words she didn't want to hear.

He returned with a mirror, which he held up, showing her a woman, her features familiar, the tilt of her nose, the fullness of her lips, but her eyes. They were all wrong. As was the vivid red hair. She'd been a ginger at best.

"Not me."

"Touch your face."

The suggestion was a good one. The mirror had to be false.

Raising a hand, she bit her lip as she saw the mirror reflect her actions.

Reflecting her.

"No." She grabbed hold of the mirror and stared, noticing the differences. No lines and yet the rounded cheeks she recalled, the freshness of her youth, had fled. "I'm old."

"You're beautiful." Said softly and yet she reacted as if he'd shouted. She flung the mirror. The crash as it broke not satisfying. She grabbed him by the shirt and once more manhandled him, drawing him close.

"You lie."

"You know I'm not."

But if he spoke the truth...

Her mind shut down rather than listen any more, unable to handle what it meant.

Adrian wouldn't leave it alone. "There's more to the story. When the hospital was going to yank the plug, I saved you and—"

Rather than listen, she did the only thing she could think of to quiet him—that didn't involve wringing his neck or roasting him over a fire. She pressed her mouth to his, meaning to suck the life from him. Pull the oxygen from his very lungs to feed the fire within. Except, the moment their lips touched her intent changed.

For one, kissing him ignited her in a strange way that had nothing to do with her internal fire. She craved the taste of his mouth. The flavor of his tongue.

She kissed him, and he kissed her back, the embrace starting out cautious then turning fierce. Hunger heated her. The kind that brought moisture between her legs and demanded satisfaction.

She thrust a hand between their bodies and cupped him. Found him hard and ready.

"Jane," he managed to mutter in between kisses. "We have to stop this, Jane."

"No." She'd stop when she was done. When he'd given her what she needed to extinguish the heat inside her.

She gripped his shirt and tore it, rending it in two then yanking it from his upper body. His skin bared to her, she explored him with her lips, feeling his surprise, his arousal, his regret.

Regret for what?

The pinch at her back had her pulling away. "Why..." she whispered before lethargy tugged at her eyelids.

The next time they opened, she stared at a ceiling as she lay in a bed.

Again!

"Bastard." The word growled from her as she rolled from the bed and hit the floor with a thump, noticing she still wore the robe and it remained dark outside. So not out for as long as the first betrayal.

A steady rhythm of thumps as he pounded down stairs. He appeared, hair tousled, his upper body shirt-less while his pants hung low off lean hips. It was almost enough to switch her anger to arousal.

Then he opened his mouth.

"Are you all right?" he asked.

"You drugged me," she accused. Drugged her because he didn't want to kiss her!

"I did. Sorry. But things were getting out of hand."

Not the answer she expected. She frowned. "The kiss was bad?"

"No, the kiss was amazing, which was the problem."

Amazing. Yet he stopped. "Good kiss."

"A very good kiss."

"I want more."

"So I gathered, but we can't."

Her nostrils flared as jealousy consumed her. "You have a woman already."

"No. I'm single. Have been for a long time actually."

Which made it even harder to understand. "Why?"

"Because I'm your doctor."

"I'm not sick." She felt fine. Better than fine. If confused. Finding out she'd lost twenty years of her life remained a shock she'd have to deal with. But at least her mind was coming back to her. Enough that she could cringe at the things she'd done since waking.

Oh my God what did I do to that vagrant under the

bridge? Before she could run to a bathroom and throw up, he was talking again.

"You're not sick, but you are recovering. Your body has been asleep for twenty years."

He kept saying that, yet she knew enough to point out a few wrong facts. "Why can I walk?" Her muscles should have atrophied.

"You were never paralyzed."

At her pointed look, he expanded. "The drug you overdosed on shut down your heart. A few other organs, too, but that was the main one. The doctors kept you on a feeding tube and respirator for a long time. Without those things you would have died. Even once I got a hold of you and began my own special treatment, you needed those things to survive. You showed no sign of brain activity."

"I was awake." Caught inside a shell. Pounding to get out, and not being heard.

"You were?" His brows lifted. Excitement hued his next rapid-fire questions. "Do you remember your time in the coma? Could you hear? Feel?"

"Yes." Her lips turned down, and he caught the despair.

"I'm sorry, Jane. That was insensitive of me. It's just, the other coma patients I've dealt with all wake up as if they'd just gone to sleep."

"Others?"

"Yes, there are more of you. You might say I

specialize in lost causes. Those that are abandoned to live out their life in a bodily prison."

"Like you," she stated, eyeing his legs then his face.

"Especially like me. I was the first to get the treatment. And as you can see..." He did a pirouette. "It is quite effective. It helped you recover."

"You gave me the same?" She frowned. "Not same problem." The sentences were flowing easier, if still a bit choppy.

"No, we suffered two different medical fates, but it turns out the cure for so many things is similar. In your case, I fine-tuned it to your needs. Thought for the longest time I'd failed, but you woke."

She'd woken in a panic, her lungs seizing with smoke, the heat around her almost unbearable. Frozen in a bed that smoldered. Things were hazy after that. A brief impression of intense warmth, an explosion, then running, always running and hiding.

"You fixed me?" More question than statement.

"I did."

"You did this." She held up her hand and lit the tip.

That brought a frown. "I don't know why you can do that. Which is why we need to run tests." His expression turned earnest. "You're special, Jane."

The words brought warmth and annoyance because he wasn't talking about her as a woman but a thing of interest. "I don't want to be different," she huffed.

"Because being different makes you an outcast. Believe me I understand." His lips turned down.

Her thoughts clearer now than ever, she understood the inadvertent insult she'd inflicted. But before she could apologize, a thump drew their attention.

"Looks like me might have company." Adrian turned from her. "Hold on a second while I deal with it."

Deal with what?

He headed for a cabinet on the wall, but she paid him no attention as the banging came again, followed by knocking as something pressed against the glass.

The misshapen face peered inside, making her gasp. "What is that?"

"An unfortunate side effect."

"Excuse me?" She whirled on him. "A side effect of what?"

"The treatment."

"He's a patient?"

"Was. Bryant chose to leave before we were done."

"He's a monster."

Slamming a cartridge into the hilt of the handgun, Adrian offered a rueful smile. "Aren't we all?"

"What does he want?"

"How would I know? If this were a horror flick, I'd say blood or brains." Adrian shrugged even as the thing in the window pounded the glass, leaving wet, slobbery streaks on it.

"He wants to kill you."

"Don't sound so surprised. You wanted to do the same, as I recall."

But she had a reason. She thought he'd hurt her. Instead, it turned out he was trying to help, and it was working. She was feeling almost back to normal, if in a new body that fascinated, the shape more defined, brimming with energy. "What are we going to do?"

"*We*," he emphasized, "are doing nothing. You're going to get something to eat while I handle Bryant."

"You can't go out there." Did he not sense the danger lurking in that thing licking the window?

"I've got this, Jane. Bryant and those broken like him are my cross to bear." That said, he closed the cabinet and strode to the sliding glass door, gun in hand.

The sight caused a moment of disconnect. *What's Adrian going to do with that gun?* The Adrian she knew fought back with words.

As Adrian approached the back wall, the thing at the window cackled loud enough to be heard and jumped excitedly. She could only watch as Adrian entered a sequence of key presses on the pad beside the door. *Beep.* The door slid open as Adrian took a few paces back.

She waited for him to talk the thing down, just like he had with her.

But he said not a word as the monster dove in —*bang*—and hit the floor as Adrian shot it in the head.

CHAPTER TWELVE

THERE WAS A MOMENT OF SILENCE AFTER BRYANT hit the floor before Jane screeched, "You killed him!"

"Yes." Adrian kept the word low as he glanced outside. He checked for more trouble before closing the door and locking it.

"You didn't even try to talk to him."

"Do you really think he would have answered?" Adrian asked, tucking the gun in the waistband of his pants.

She eyed him. Not his face. But his body. Her gaze tracking over his skin and lower, bringing an arousal that his tight underwear hopefully hid. As a teenager, she had fueled more than one erotic fantasy, and now as an adult, she was more alluring than ever.

She frowned. "I was out of it when I attacked you, but you didn't shoot me."

"I knew you weren't a lost cause." More like hoped, because he had a feeling she was his only hope.

"How could you know that? I came here to kill you," she insisted.

He sighed and raked fingers through his hair. "What would you like me to tell you, Jane? Did I hesitate with you? Yes, I fucking did, which was dumb. Trust me, Jett has told me a couple of times now that I should have either locked you up or shot you by now."

"Who's Jett?" she growled.

"My right-hand man. One of the few left. And not the subject at hand. I am not the boy you remember. You've yet to truly meet the man. I will, however, say this; I won't hesitate to do what has to be done."

"Killing patients?" Her gaze flicked to the one on the floor. "Hiding evidence of what you did."

"The world isn't ready for what I can offer yet." They might never be ready. Or even understand. He'd crossed so many lines in his pursuit of a cure. Trampled on people's rights and feelings. Destroyed those who didn't follow his vision.

Only now did he feel some remorse. But at the same time, he'd do it all again—especially if it meant saving Jane.

"What went wrong with his treatment?" she asked, the curiosity in her query a surprise.

"Bryant was a different case than both of us. He was in a bad helicopter crash. Lost both legs and an arm. Suffered a severe brain injury and burns over sixty percent of his body."

Her nose wrinkled, possibly due to the potent stench filling the basement. "He doesn't look burned. He has a lot of hair."

His lips twitched. "Because, in order to regenerate surface skin, we had to blend his DNA with one that would reconstitute it."

"I don't understand."

"It's complicated, and I want to tell you all about it, but I really need to get rid of this." He waved a hand at the cooling corpse.

"You going to eat it?"

For a moment his hunger flared and demanded meat. His lip curled back over his teeth before he managed a barked, "Of course not!" The very fact she asked, though, made him wonder...had she eaten human flesh? And of even more interest, how did it taste?

Before he could ask her to spark the barbecue and pull out some spices, he came to his senses. "We don't eat people, Jane." Said in his sternest voice.

It didn't stop the curve of her lips. "Now that's a right shame. I would have taken you for a man who liked to give and receive."

The flirting threw him off balance. "You know what I mean."

"Yes. It appears you still lack a sense of humor."

He pointed to the body. "This isn't exactly funny."

"No. It's not. It's very odd as a matter of fact. How did he know you lived here? Did the shadow tell him, too?"

"What shadow?"

She pressed her lips tight.

"Jane..." he cajoled.

"When you left the city, someone, I never saw their face, pointed me in your direction."

"You had help?"

"Of a sort. But then, once I got going, I just knew where to go." She shrugged. "Maybe it's your magnetic personality?"

"Ha. Ha. Very funny." But possibly true. "Did you know it was me you were coming to find?"

Again, her shoulders rolled. "Not exactly. I just remember being mad. And you being the source of that anger."

"Everyone's mad," he grumbled. "Some days, I really wish I'd stopped at just curing myself."

"But then I wouldn't be here." The soft answer brought his gaze.

"No. You wouldn't. So the real question is, do the ends justify my actions?"

"Who says justification is needed? We are all thinking creatures capable of choice. Who's to say your choice is wrong, or someone else's right?" Her lips curved. "Do rules created by others really apply to an individual?"

"That's some deep thinking, Jane. And probably

not the right time for it. I've got to get this out of here."
He waved a hand to the body, wishing he could talk
more at length with her. The very fact she could
discourse and even make intellectual and moral argu-
ment was fascinating.

But if there was one rule in every mad scientist's
book, it was "get rid of the body." The quicker, the
better.

She stretched. "Party pooper." The arch of her
back thrust out her chest, and he looked away.

He needed space. Time to regroup and marshal his
thoughts. "Listen, while I get this handled, why don't
you go have a hot bath. I've got a soaker tub with—" He
never got to say jets. Jane squealed and took off.

He hoped it was a long one. Which led to him
thinking of her, naked, in his bathroom, in his tub...

He stared at the dead body until the erection left.

Luckily, the cleaning crew arrived quickly to
handle his newest mess. He'd thought about setting the
corpse alight. However, given Jane was likely to dance
on the body as it burned, and perhaps even have a
nibble, he decided against it.

Best get rid of it.

While the cleaners never asked questions—just
invoiced him an ungodly amount—he expected Jane
would have plenty of things to say after her bath. Now
that she'd become aware again, she was bright. Inquisitive. Way too fucking gorgeous.

He still remembered the feel of her mouth on his.

The heat of her body. The desire that almost had him taking her, his one moral rule be damned.

But it was her heat that ultimately stopped him because the scientist in him wondered if she'd burn him alive once he sank balls deep into her.

Funny how the possibility excited, which, in turn, led to him doing the right thing and putting her to sleep.

Right? Ha. You should have fucked her.

Odd how that voice sounded like his.

He used the cleanup time to try and plan his next move. Even his next words. For the moment, Jane had stopped arguing that reality was but a dream. Which meant the truth he still had to impart would hit her hard. He'd yet to tell her about her parents. Nor had she thought to inquire about Benedict. And while she knew he'd cured her, she had yet to ask the most obvious—*what did I do to her?*

The cleaners no sooner left, their van ironically labeled Pest Removal, than Jett arrived, with Becky in tow. The smart man at least knew to come bearing breakfast from Tim Horton's: a tray of coffees hot enough to still steam in the air and, in his wife's hands, a box of treats.

"Where is she?" his former nursing assistant asked. Becky looked good this morning, her skin fresh and her eyes bright. Better than a few weeks ago when they'd had to start her on some supplements—in the tub.

Apparently pregnant mermaids needed water nutrients as much as human vitamins.

"Jane is still scalding herself in the tub." He jerked a thumb over his shoulder indicating the inside of the house.

"I can't believe you doped her again." Becky huffed, having obviously gotten the latest details from Jett.

"She didn't give me a choice." When she'd kissed him, all he'd wanted was to kiss her back. And not just on her mouth. He panicked. Rather than push her away and explain how inappropriate it was, he'd drugged her.

Pathetic.

"Pathetic!" Becky more or less read his mind as she slapped his arm. "Just like a guy to dart first and talk later. I thought you said she could be reasoned with."

"She thinks what's happening is a dream." He didn't mention the part where he was pretty sure he'd convinced her otherwise.

Becky exclaimed, "More like a nightmare."

"Gee thanks," was Jett's sarcastic retort.

"I wasn't talking about our situation," Becky huffed at her husband with a roll of her eyes, stepping into the house and peeling off her outer layer. "Think of it from Jane's point of view. She's been asleep for two decades. She wakes up and finds out that not only did she OD, and lose out on half her life, but her parents are dead and you experimented on her."

"What do you mean experimented?" screeched by a Jane who overheard. "I thought you gave me a cure."

Meeting her accusing stare, he didn't cower. "I did give you a cure. It's just not exactly approved by any agencies yet."

"And what of my parents?" she snapped. "Where are they?"

"I thought you understood they died when I took over your care."

Judging by her angry expression? No, she hadn't.

"Asshole!" A growled insult followed by the slam of a door.

Becky gave him an incredulous look. "I thought you told her everything."

"Not quite. There was a lot to cover." Adrian rubbed at the knot on his forehead, the throb becoming familiar.

"You are such a man!" Becky declared before stomping off in Jane's direction, only to have Jett snare her arm.

"Where are you going?" he asked.

"To talk to her, of course."

Adrian cleared his throat. "Um, that might not be a safe idea."

"What he said," Jett added.

"You saying I can't handle myself?" Becky pulled free of her husband and crossed her arms, her expression daring them to challenge her. Gone was the broken nurse he'd hired, in her place a feisty woman who, when riled, bristled with scales.

"I'm saying you're a lover not a fighter. That woman could kill you before you even said hello." Jett doubled down.

"If she was going to kill someone, she'd have killed him." Becky jabbed a finger in Adrian's direction. While they'd come to a truce after the unfortunate incident where he was going to sell Becky for quick cash, she still didn't like him. As for Jett, he grasped business. And his business was keeping his wife happy.

"She probably doesn't want to twist off his head yet just in case she still needs him for something. But she might not feel the same about you," Jett retorted.

"Guess I'm not getting boss of the year again," Adrian muttered.

"If you want a trophy for biggest asshole, I'm pretty sure you'll win hands down," Becky shouted as she headed for the kitchen.

Left alone with Jett, Adrian sighed. "Go ahead. Tell me how I'm doing everything wrong."

A snort met his statement. "I'd have said that was obvious. But, at the same time, while you did a lot of questionable shit, without you acting out your god complex, I wouldn't have met my wife. So..." Jett shrugged.

"There are days I ask myself if it was worth it." In a rare moment of truth, Adrian admitted, "I could have stopped once I cured myself." Could have stopped any step of the way.

"If you had, Becky would have died of her cancer by now."

He cast a glance at Jett. "I didn't so much cure her as change her."

"Yep. You did. But I'd rather Red be able to harangue us both, even if sometimes she has to resort to spitting water at me from the tub."

Adrian's lips quirked. "She's a firecracker."

"Most redheads are. Keep that in mind." Jett didn't need to say anything more.

Adrian's gaze flicked down the hall. "Jane's doing extremely well given circumstances."

"Don't really give a rat's ass about Jane. How are you doing?" Jett asked.

The very act of asking startled Adrian. "I'm fine."

"Are you?" Jett headed for the patio doors and looked outside, his gaze keen and searching. "You killed again."

"Jealous?" Because it used to be Jett that dealt with his messes.

"No, but I am wondering why you've chosen to kill so much of late."

Wasn't it obvious? "They're not giving me much of a choice," spoken a touch defensively.

"Not judging," Jett remarked, glancing at him briefly over his shoulder. "But the old Adrian I knew was about helping and healing. He would have armed himself with tranquilizers. Whereas new Adrian has been eliminating his patients."

"I didn't kill Jane."

"The exception. Everyone else is getting a quick bullet to the head."

"Because that's the quickest way to deal with someone intent on murder."

"Jane came here to murder your ass, and yet you doped her instead of sending her on to her final destination."

"Jane's different." For so many reasons.

"No, she's not. You're different. With her, you have compassion. A willingness to help. But not so much with anyone else that shows up at your door—or window." He turned from the sliding pane to face Adrian.

"Jane responded to my words."

"Because you gave her words. The thing you just dispatched got a quick bullet to the head."

How did Jett know? He'd taken away his security camera access. Apparently, not as well as he'd thought.

Adrian pressed his lips. "You've been spying on me."

"Yep." No attempt at denial. Jett's hard, flat gaze fixed him. "And don't expect an apology for it. I need you alive for my wife and the babies she's carrying. Yet, you seem determined to do stupid thing after stupid thing. If you're suicidal, it might be quicker to jump off something high. Or run into my fist a few times." Jett held it up.

"You are insubordinate for an employee."

"Good thing we're past that."

"Don't tell me we're friends," Adrian said with disdain to hide the clenching in his chest.

"Fuck no."

The expected answer, so why did Adrian not like it? He changed the subject. "When is Luke bringing Margaret back? I received all the supplies we should need."

"Soon. He says Margaret wants to get some stuff ready before the birth of the baby."

"She's nesting," Adrian stated, having spent his down time doing research on pregnancy and birth—for humans and wolves. He believed it best to cover all his bases.

"Sounds like something birds do." Jett grimaced.

"It's a need many expectant mothers feel that leads them to preparing the home for the arrival of an infant."

"Is that why Becky keeps harassing me to get more shit for the nursery?"

"Are you talking smack about the babies?" Becky appeared suddenly, rounded tummy leading the way. She held a stack of small plates with the donut box perched on top.

She wasn't alone. At her back stood Jane, her

expression angry, especially when she glared at Adrian, but she'd not fled.

A step in the right direction.

"Donuts anyone?" Becky asked, dumping the dishes and treats on the living room table. She didn't wait for takers, loading a plate with a pair of pastries and snaring a cup from the tray.

Adrian frowned. "Caffeine might not be a good idea given the pregnancy."

Eyeing him over the steaming rim, Becky smiled, and managed to give him a middle finger. "This is not the Middle Ages. One cup a day won't hurt."

"Is there sugar?" Jane asked, coming close enough to grab a cup of her own.

"You want the one labeled diabetes in a cup," Jett jested, pointing to the large one labeled ten S. As in ten sugars. He really had been watching.

As for Adrian...he was left with the one dangling a string. He held it up and glared at his employee. "Tea?"

"Coffee makes you irritable."

For some reason this made Jane giggle.

There was silence for several minutes as they munched on donuts and sipped warm drinks.

Meddling Becky was the one to first shatter that peace. "Sorry Adrian is such a dick."

He choked on his mouthful of tea. Jane outright laughed and Jett—that fucker—tried hard not to grin.

"Is the name-calling necessary?" Adrian sputtered.

Becky's hands lifted in surrender. "Hey, I'm not the one who kept secrets."

"It wasn't a secret. I just hadn't had time yet to broach those things," he mumbled.

Jane jumped to his defense. "It wasn't his fault. Things have been a touch"—she paused, searching for a word—"complicated since I woke."

"Woke and came looking for the boss man." Jett leaned against the fireplace, coffee in hand. "Thought for sure you were gonna kill him that first night. When you lifted him by the throat and his eyes were bulging, thought he was a goner for sure." Jett mimed choking then laughed. "I might get that put on a card for the holidays."

Adrian's sharp glare did nothing to stop his guard from speaking with impudence. But it was hard to stay mad when Jane reacted with a mischievous smile.

"You never know, I might still choke him like a chicken," Jane joked. "But before I do that, I need to know more about what happened. Everything this time." The suspicious statement was aimed at him.

Becky, having polished off her donuts, jumped in. "In a nutshell? You were in a coma. He healed you. And like everyone else that got his treatment, there are side effects." Becky was matter-of-fact.

"What kind of side effects?" Jane asked.

Here came the part that made Adrian almost squirm in his seat. While living rather than dying was obviously the biggest benefit, sometimes the genetic melds took a little too well and the person became...less than a person.

Like you, boyo. What are you now? Man? Monster?
Shut up.

"The side effects vary." Becky shrugged. "But there is always something. Fur. Fangs. Wings. A tail, sometimes two. Fins. Got any of that?"

"Not exactly." The hesitance showed as Jane hedged.

Adrian cleared his throat. "Many of the patients show no outwards signs, as you well know." Look at him, perfect on the outside.

But you're a mess inside, boyo.

"Yeah, some look normal, but many more turn into complete monsters." Becky addressed Adrian with a stern glare. "Let's not pretend otherwise."

"That depends on your definition of monster."

Jett lowered his coffee long enough to mutter, "Thing that kills people and eats them."

"Meat is meat."

Adrian almost choked on his coffee as Jane replied. Not exactly a human answer, but the expression on Jett's face? Now that was worthy of a Christmas card.

Becky diverted attention. "Jeezus, someone is doing back flips in there." She put a hand to her stomach, drawing attention to the growing size of her belly. Not unusual given she did carry twins; however, he'd have to watch her even more closely given the quick gestation and the size of the baby seen in Margaret.

Jane eyed the pregnant hump with interest. Which gave Adrian an idea.

He clapped his hands and said, "Who wants to see the babies in Becky's tummy?"

With a squeal, Becky heaved herself off the couch. "You got the ultrasound machine?"

"I did. It's downstairs."

"In the bad place," Jane muttered. "He makes me sleep down there."

"Because it's the only place with a bed," was his retort. Most of the main floor comprised of his living area and master bedroom.

Jett led the way, his hand guiding Becky in the middle of her back, which left Adrian with Jane, who sidled close and said, "Your bed is big enough for two."

What was that supposed to mean?

Idiot. What do you think it means?

She wanted to share his bed. For sleep only? Something else? How confusing.

He stumbled after them, mind spinning, and almost missed her next statement.

"My parents are really dead."

"Yes. I'm sorry."

She paused in the stairs, forcing him to pause, too. "Why? You didn't know them."

"Because you're probably sad."

She cocked her head as if in thought. "Yes and no. In many ways, they're like a dream. A pleasant one that's faded into the background."

"They loved you very much. When the doctors wanted to take you off the respirator, they refused. They kept you alive." A good thing, because at eighteen he didn't have the means or ability to do anything to help her.

"My mom visited me a lot." Her eyes took on a dreamy cast. "She read to me. And then she was gone. But the weird thing is..." She focused on him. "Other people started reading, too."

The revelation startled. "That would be the audio books I had the nursing staff play for you. Podcasts, too. Since I wasn't sure how much you could hear or feel, I covered all the bases." He kept her to what would have been a normal wake and sleep cycle. Feedings at breakfast, noon, and dinnertime. A massage four times a day to keep her muscles supple. A blend of music, books, and current news played to her daily. Lights off at night with the curtains opened in the day to bathe her in sunlight. Temperature control ensuring she didn't get too hot. Which, in retrospect, might have delayed her recovery.

"Did Trump truly become the president?" she asked.

"Yes, and this is a phone." He held up his smartphone and watched her eyes widen in wonder. She grabbed it and turned it over in her hands, gasping when the screen lit.

"It's so small." But her amazement was huge.

There was so much he wanted to show her. If she'd let him.

"Hello, impatient pregnant woman threating bodily harm if you don't get down here," Jett shouted.

"We'd better go," he said, wanting to throttle Jett. For just a second, he and Jane had shared a real moment. A connection.

He would have liked to savor it longer, because he had a feeling it wouldn't last once she truly grasped the extent of his experiments.

CHAPTER THIRTEEN

ADRIAN WENT AHEAD OF JANE, GIVING HER HIS back. His trust.

It would be so easy to kill him.

Kill him for what? Saving her? If not for him, she'd be six feet underground. He'd cared for her even though he didn't have to. Watched over her. Why?

Entering the basement, which in his defense was nothing like a cell with its big windows and ample light, she glared at her bed. Freshly made with new sheets. The body on the floor gone, along with the mess it made.

She still recalled that stunning moment when Adrian shot the creature.

Pop. No hesitation nor any hint of regret on his face. She'd heard him arguing with that man. Jett. Saying he had no real choice. The *thing* attacked him. But Jett raised a good point. She'd also tried to kill him.

He could have shot me. Instead, he invited her into his home. Bought her gifts. She glanced down at the light gray tracksuit, the material soft and supple, the shoes almost like slippers with their flexibility. He made her food. Provided bath salts that she might have a luxurious soak. No cold water in the tub, just pure hot. Hot enough to scald a person, which meant her ability to withstand and luxuriate in it must be a side effect of the cure he'd given her. Less a side effect and more a superpower. But given he was the doctor who'd created it, did that make him the villain?

Jane almost barked at the woman who clambered onto her bed. Hadn't she just bitched a few minutes ago that she didn't want it? Yet already she considered it hers. As to Adrian's blithe reply that it was the only other bed available? She'd certainly not seen another upstairs other than his.

A gentleman would have offered it. And she would have said no. Which meant...nothing in the grand scheme of things. Her world had suddenly erupted, and she was straggling to catch up, looking for ways to vent at the unfairness of it all.

In that maelstrom of confusion, there was only one thing that provided a stable point.

As Jett tended his wife, she sidled close to Adrian's side and murmured, "From now on, I think I should get the bed, and you get the one on wheels."

He barely cast her a glance, intent on getting his machine going. "I'll have you know, the mattress I use down here is of the highest quality. The sheets an expensive Egyptian cotton blend."

"I'm glad you like it so much, because you'll be sleeping on it."

"What happened to sharing the big one in my room?" Said with a devilish tilt of his brow.

Before she could reply, he was moving away from her, the machine rolling with him.

Rather than ogle Becky's gigantic belly, Jane prowled the room, a little miffed when he didn't pay her any mind. Nope, Adrian was intent on dumping goop on another woman and rubbing her flesh with it.

Jane huffed out some smoke and realized she needed to get a grip. Her jealousy was unwarranted on many fronts. For one, the gal's husband was standing right there and would kill Adrian if he tried anything. And two, she didn't care who Adrian rubbed.

She just kind of wished he'd rub her.

"Say hello to the twins." Adrian's words drew her attention to the screen he was using, nothing so basic as a two dimensional black and white swirl no one understood. This was state-of-the-art equipment that must be malfunctioning because on screen it looked like a pair of tadpoles were swimming and darting.

"What are those?" she asked, drawing near.

Becky replied softly, "My babies."

"But they're..." She trailed off rather than say what she really thought.

Her hesitation didn't go unnoticed. Jett replied, his

words emerging gruff and challenging. "Yes, those are our babies, and yes, they're a little different than you'd expect. What you might call one of those side effects we were talking about."

Jane shot Becky a sharp look. "You're Adrian's patient, too?"

She nodded. "More or less."

"And the cure screwed up the babies?" She was blunt, partially due to shock and also because she wanted to understand.

"That's a harsh assessment. We won't really be able to judge until the children are born," Adrian said.

She turned an incredulous gaze on him. "She has a pair of baby frogs swimming in her belly."

"I assure you, they are not frogs, even if it appears some of the amphibian characteristics Becky imbibed crossed over to the fetuses."

"You fed her frog DNA?" Jane couldn't help her disgust, which was probably why Jett snapped.

"I wouldn't act so high and mighty, Little Miss Firestarter. Why don't you ask him what animals you've got running around inside?"

"Me?" Her eyes rounded as she stared at Adrian. "Did you mess with my DNA, too?"

"Yes." He held her gaze. "You don't have any amphibian genes. However, there is a bit of reptile, avian, and a few others that I'd have to check my notes for. I had to be innovative when you didn't respond to any of the treatments."

For some reason, when Adrian had spoken of fixing her, she'd not truly grasped it. She assumed he'd used conventional medicine, despite the strange ability for fire she now commanded. But it was becoming clear he'd resorted to something forbidden.

What did he do to me?

Panic fluttered in her breast, and her breathing went short.

No one noticed. Jett held Becky's hand and shared a soft look with her. Adrian was focused on the ultrasound itself. No one saw the panic in Jane, which meant she had time to calm down and regroup, gather her thoughts enough that she blurted out, "You played god with lives."

"Hardly a god. I'm a doctor, Jane. I heal."

"Don't try and play this down." Her lip curled over her teeth. "You pulled a Dr. Moreau on us."

The claim drew his steady gaze, but no apology or refute. "I wondered if it was a good idea to play that audiobook to you while you slept. I'd hoped when you woke it would help you understand because he was part of my inspiration. But whereas he experimented to create new types of beings, I did it to heal."

"Which makes it okay?" she asked sourly.

He sidestepped. "It was never my intention to change a person's humanity."

"Yet you didn't stop once you did," she conjectured.

Becky answered for him. "A good thing he didn't. If it weren't for Adrian, I'd be dead."

That drew her attention. "Were you in a coma, too?"

Becky sat up and shook her head. "Lung cancer. I had months, maybe only even weeks, to live when I went to work at Adrian's clinic."

"You experimented on your employees," she accused. Bad enough he'd done it to Jane without verbal permission, but the people he worked with, who trusted him?

"Adrian didn't do this to me. I did this to me." Becky lifted her chin defiantly. "I was dying, and he had a cure. I didn't have time to wait for human trials and the years it takes for new drugs to get approved. So I stole the cure and took it."

Eyeing her up and down, rudely, but Jane didn't care. She blurted out, "You look normal even if the babies don't."

"Give it a few hours. By tonight I'll be in our tub, spending the evening underwater. I'm a mermaid."

"Bullshit." The expletive had Jane slapping her hand over her mouth. For a moment she felt like a young girl swearing in front of the grownups. Except she was a grownup.

Becky smirked. "I think you meant to say unbeliev-able, but I assure you, it's quite true."

"But...But...You look...normal." But then again, so did Jane mostly.

"I don't grow a tail or anything, but when I submerge and breathe water, my skin does get scaly, and I can talk to fish."

"Seriously?" While some people might have been horrified, Jane was fascinated. As a young girl, she'd been obsessed with mermaids. Watched the Disney movie over and over. Decorated her room in seashells and fishy decals. If someone had told her she could actually become one, she would have said yes without hesitation. "Do you like it?"

Becky shrugged. "It is what it is. Would I prefer to have more control over when I need to go for a dip? Yes. Am I happy to be alive? Very. Would I make it go away if I could?" Again, her shoulders rolled. "I don't know. I went from being a regular kind of girl—"

"As if you'd be anything so bland," her husband muttered.

"—to the very first mermaid in existence."

"Secret mermaid," her husband amended.

"Why secret?" Jane asked.

"No one knows which is for the best. Can you imagine what kind of circus my life would be otherwise?" Becky arched a brow. "It's not about fame and fortune for me. It's my life. Now also your life, because, like me, you're different."

Those words resonated in Jane's head for a while, even after Becky and her husband left, ushered out by Adrian, who then spent time in his lab, doing science-y shit.

Ignoring her. Giving her space. Except she didn't want space. She wanted answers. After spending time watching television, which only confused her further about this new world, then eating until she could eat no more, she finally gave in and hustled down to Adrian's lair. Jane found him intent on a computer screen; however the tenseness of his back showed he was very aware of her presence.

"Did you need something, Jane?"

Rather than stall, she said bluntly, "What am I?"

"Extraordinary."

Not the answer expected, and she blinked, silenced by the one word.

He swiveled on his stool. "But that's not what you're really asking. You want to know how you've changed. What you've become. The problem is there really is no answer to that because you're unique."

"I'm a fluke. A freak. Because of you!" she accused.

He took the blame. "Yes. It is my fault because I was determined to help you."

"Why me? Why help me?"

"You needed it."

"So do hundreds of other people. I might not have all your medical knowledge, but I'm sure I heard somewhere that most cures, like stem cells"—the knowledge welling up from inside her—"work better on people with a fresh injury."

"You are correct. But that doesn't mean a doctor should just give up."

"You said I was a vegetable. How long? How long before you could even try?" How long since her parents' deaths?

"A decade in a coma ward and then another in my care, asleep."

She felt that fluttery panic again as she realized how much of her life she'd lost. She whirled from him, not wanting him to see her agitation as she fought not to explode at the unfairness of it all. "How could you all do that to me? You. My parents. You're the reason I was a prisoner in my body. You should have let me go."

"I couldn't let you die."

"Why not?" She faced him, her expression pleading. "Why try and save me?"

"Because." He pressed his lips into a firm line.

"That's not an answer. Trying is you doing it for a few years and then throwing in the towel. You took care of me for a decade. Becky says you kept me in your condo. Not with the other patients. Why?"

He shrugged and wouldn't look at her. The brash man unable to reply. Which could only mean one thing.

"You did it because you had a crush on me." She'd kind of guessed when they were together in high school but accepted it as her due back then. Jane was the popular girl who had it all. Looks. Grades. Acceptance to a university on the coast. She didn't have time for the crippled boy crushing on her from his wheelchair. Why would she? She was dating the star of the football team. The very shallowness of it made her ashamed in the here and now.

I led him on. Her acts of kindness and subtle flirting obviously something he'd taken seriously.

"You were my friend. I cared about you," he said carefully. "I felt bad about what happened."

"It wasn't your fault I was stupid and popped those pills."

"No, but I'm the reason why you overdosed. Those blue pills Benedict shared were mine."

CHAPTER FOURTEEN

"WHAT DO YOU MEAN THEY WERE YOUR PILLS?" Jane's query emerged slowly. He wanted to dig a hole and bury himself in it, knowing that any progress he'd made with her was about to come to a halt.

"The pills you overdosed on were mine. Benedict stole them." Which didn't absolve Adrian of the guilt. It came rushing at him like a tidal wave, making him regret for the millionth time his actions that night.

"You need to explain." She crossed her arms and regarded him with a flat expression. Her lips pressed into an uncompromising line.

Soon that look would turn to hate. Because he was the reason she'd ended up in a coma for too long.

"Remember prom night?" He glanced down at his hands, the fingers long and supple, unlike the gnarled claws of his teen years.

"As if I could forget."

Heat flushed his cheeks at her dry retort. "Benedict cornered me."

The bigger guy had done more than that, and it didn't start with prom.

Adrian dropped into the past as he spoke, that day living infamously in his mind.

June twenty-first. After exams and a Friday. The weather pleasant this time of year. Not too hot. The skies expected to be clear. A perfect night for prom, which Adrian had planned to spend at home, but his foster parents insisted he not miss out on an iconic rite of teen passage. The fact he couldn't wait to graduate and get out of school didn't factor into their idyllic vision of how high school should be.

His foster parents, bless their hearts—as Mrs. Kline used to say at least five times a day—remembered it as a special time. Full of friendship and laughter. They didn't have to deal with the bullying, the snide remarks, the difficulty in getting around. The loneliness...

But since they seemed so intent on the idea of him going to prom, Adrian agreed, which was how he found himself dressed in a tuxedo, his wheelchair all shiny and clean. After they dropped him off, taking pictures that he later burned, he wheeled himself inside, for the most part unremarked. He parked by a wall and watched as everyone else had fun.

There was food he didn't dare eat out of fear his hand would spasm and spill it on his tux. He didn't drink either. Just stared and envied the able-bodied.

Look at them dancing after dinner. The girls shimmying their hips, their lips spread in wide smiles. Check out the guys, some of them doing a simple two-step shuffle, but others actually had some groove.

Everyone looked their best. This was their shining moment. They'd spent twelve years in school to get the rinky-dink diploma that called them a graduate. A good chunk of them would now go to college or university. Others would enter the workforce.

Adrian would be going away. A full scholarship from a university that was known to accept diverse students and was particularly pleased to snare one with his remarkable grades. He was sure his life would be about the same. Lonely. Because who wanted to be friends with the cripple? Which, as it turned out, was a high school thing. Once he got among his intellectual peers, no one cared about his body. His mind was his best attribute. But that was later.

On prom night, he was less than a wallflower. Despite the armor he'd used to protect himself over the years, it hurt to watch people he'd known a good chunk of his life having fun with no thought to the boy in the chair. Inclusivity in many ways was just a word. Sure, people said hi to him. The school took its fair share of photo ops to show they were progressive, but in the end, when it came to life...he was always sitting in the shadows.

Unlike Benedict. The guy strutted in as if all eyes should be on him, and many were. If the school hadn't abolished it, the star of the football team would have surely been crowned king with Jane as his lovely queen. She certainly looked regal in her off-the-shoulder gown made of some shimmery gold material that brought out the fine porcelain of her skin. She'd sprinkled glitter in her auburn hair, the long locks curled and left loose. The strands shimmied when she danced with Benedict. Her hand clutched at his shoulder as he dipped her and drew a bark of laughter. Her perfect full, red lips gasped when Benedict dared to cup her ass. Treating Jane like a whore in front of everyone. Flaunting the fact he was sleeping with the sexiest girl in school.

How Adrian hated that bastard.

But it wasn't just because Benedict got to be with the girl Adrian adored. It was the name-calling. The bullying. The dog shit left on the front walk that he had to roll through to get to his special needs bus. So many incidents that culminated in the final straw a few days before in the school bathroom. Adrian was about to take his pain meds, the spasms being particularly vicious that day, when Benedict barreled in, his raucous laughter the equivalent of nails on chalkboard.

"If it isn't my favorite cripple. How's it going, Wheelie?"

Adrian had learned that replying only prolonged the misery. His only hope was someone else would come in before Benedict got rough.

"What's that you got there?

Adrian never even thought to hide the pill bottle in the palm of his hand.

"Oh ho. Wheelie's popping pills. How come you aren't sharing?"

"These are for my illness," he finally spat.

"I thought you couldn't be fixed."

"I can't." And he tired of people asking him if there was any hope. He had none. "I take these to manage my pain."

Too late, he understood his mistake.

"Well shit, Wheelie. You've been holding out on me. All this time you've had the good stuff." Benedict snapped his fingers. "Hand it over."

"No." Adrian clamped his hand down. "These are prescription." Which meant the pharmacist and his doctor counted every one. It wouldn't do for the sick boy to become addicted.

Refusing only meant Benedict pried open his hand and stole the one thing that made the discomfort bearable.

Benedict hunted him down the next day for more and the next. Having to show up for his exams meant Adrian couldn't avoid him.

And Adrian had no doubt Benedict would come after him again tonight. After all, prom was the night for teens to go wild. Sex, alcohol, drugs... Was it any wonder every year there was a tragedy on what should be the most triumphant of nights?

But perhaps Adrian wouldn't have to worry.

After all, Benedict never once looked his way. Just when Adrian was thinking he'd stayed long enough for his foster parents to be happy, Benedict left Jane by the drink table to exit the building with a bunch of his friends. Probably going to smoke some dope in the parking lot. It made Adrian want to call in an anonymous tip to the university that took Benedict on a football scholarship.

Jane scooped a glass of punch. Then a second one.

To his surprise, she strolled toward him, a goddess in the flesh who looked right at Adrian and smiled.

"Hey," she said. "You came."

"Yeah." He almost did once her perfume hit him.

"Drink?" She held out the glass, and he couldn't say no.

He grabbed it, willing his hand to behave. Then realized he needed to say something. "You look"—amazing, beautiful, jaw dropping—*"good."*

It was apparently enough because she beamed at him. "Thanks."

An awkward silence fell, mostly because he was too tongue-tied to say anything.

"Wanna dance?" The query from her surprised him.

Angered him a bit, too. Was she making fun of him now as well? "I can't," he snapped.

"Of course, you can." To his shock, she grabbed the glass and put it aside before she sat on his lap. He might have stopped breathing. Surprise. Pleasure. Way too much pleasure stole his voice.

Jane placed her hand on the controls for his chair, sending them into a lurching spin. She laughed. "Oops. Maybe you should be in charge."

He'd do anything she wanted if she stayed on his lap. He spun them in his chair, doing a quick left and right, a full triple spin that had her clutching at him. Her laughter brushing over his skin. The moment well worth the barked, "What the fuck you doing with my girlfriend, Wheelie?"

Rising with a giggle, Jane put her hand on Benedict's chest. "Calm down. I was the one who wanted to dance." She cast a glance over her shoulder. "Adrian was kind enough to humor me."

"I'm sure he was," grumbled the athlete.

"Grab me another drink, and then we can have our own dance." She waggled her glass at her boyfriend, who snatched it and stomped off.

Adrian wished the guy would drop dead.

"He doesn't know it yet, but I'm breaking up with him before end of summer." She glanced at Adrian. "Fresh start at university and all."

The news elated him. "You deserve better."

"Why, Adrian, are you flirting with me?" She winked. "I'd better go before he comes back beating his chest. Thank you for the dance." She leaned down and, before he could grasp her intent, kissed his cheek.

He sat there stunned. Benedict's glower had no power to remove his euphoric state.

She kissed me.

And then she went to slow dance with another guy, who seemed determined to show the world she was his. His hands were less than discreet. The kissing X-rated. When Adrian could no longer stand watching, he exited the ballroom—which, on a daily basis, served as the community center. A cheaper alternative to the expensive hotel options in the city.

His foster father had said to call when he needed a ride, but Adrian wanted some quiet time to himself. He quickly left the raucous boom boom *of the music behind, the only sound the whir of the motor in his wheelchair.*

And footsteps.

Possibly just another person going home.

But by the pit in his stomach, he knew. Knew even before the drawled, "Oh, Wheelie. I think you forgot something."

Adrian knew he wouldn't have the speed, but he tried to move faster anyhow. It just wasn't enough to escape. Benedict sprang in front of him, bumping his chair. "Leaving so soon, Wheelie? I thought you'd try and stick around, maybe cop another feel of my girlfriend."

"I didn't touch her."

"But you wanted to."

Yes. Yes, he did. Instead Adrian blurted out, "You don't deserve her."

"And you do?" Benedict laughed. "Jane doesn't

need a cripple. She wants a man." He grabbed his crotch.

"If she wants a man, then what is she doing with you?" It was like taunting a bull. But Adrian didn't care.

"Little fucker." He was hauled out of his chair by the hands gripping his coat. Benedict didn't hit him though. "Think you're so tough. Let's see you get up." Adrian found himself propelled to the ground, barely having time to put out his hands.

He still hit hard, smacking his face on the pavement. The pain radiated immediately, but Benedict wasn't done. He rolled Adrian over and began tearing at him. Not hitting but going through his pockets until he found what he was looking for.

Adrian's stash of meds.

"Now we've got a party." Benedict shook the bottle. "Happy graduation, motherfucker!"

It occurred to Adrian he could tell Benedict those weren't opioids he'd stolen but some newly prescribed medication—with a stern warning to avoid alcohol—to help him handle the seizures. But as he crawled to his chair, watching Benedict's strut, he kept that knowledge to himself.

I hope that bastard ends up drooling in a hospital. It would serve him right.

Only a few days later, when he heard the story of what happened to Benedict and Jane, did he wish he'd acted differently.

"I should have said something instead of letting him walk away with my seizure meds thinking they were opioids."

Jane had barely blinked while he told his story, the basic parts at any rate. She didn't need to know about his boner when she'd sat on him.

"You killed Benedict," she muttered.

"Not intentionally."

"You killed him, and almost killed me," she seethed, her eyes beginning to glow.

"I didn't know you'd take the drugs, too." He never ever would have thought that Jane would pop them. Or take them with alcohol. When he'd found out, he was horrified. And scared, convinced the cops would appear at any moment to arrest him. Surely, they'd recovered his pill bottle?

But as the days then weeks passed, and summer marched into fall, no one came, and Adrian went off to school.

And became the man he was today.

Slap. "Because of you I spent twenty years in a coma!" she shrieked. The heat of her rage surely left an imprint on his cheek.

"I'm sorry." The only thing left to say.

"Sorry doesn't give me back my life!" She stalked to the sliding glass door. "Open it."

"Jane."

"Don't fucking talk to me right now. I am so mad."

He could tell. She literally smoked.

"I've been trying to make amends."

"How? By experimenting on me?" she spat. "Making me into some monster thing?"

"You're not a monster."

"Says the mad scientist who created me," she mocked.

"You forget, I gave the cure to myself first."

"But did you lose the best years of your life? Did you get to go to college? Date? Get drunk legally when you turned twenty-one? I didn't. Nor was I there when my parents died. I missed everything."

"You have a second chance now. I'll set you up with money. You can do—"

She slashed her hand through the air. "I don't want anything from you." She turned from him and placed her hands on the glass. Even from where he sat, he could feel the heat, see it as glass rippled and melted.

She shoved through it as if it were taffy and in moments was gone.

Taking his only hope of sanity and happiness with her.

CHAPTER FIFTEEN

He stole my life!

The truth hit Jane like a bomb. Exploding her mind. Shattering it. And Jane had to escape. Had to run from the man lest she kill him.

She barely grasped how she managed to get out of the house. Rage heated her and helped her find a way. Soon she was running in the forest, her body a flaming brand of betrayal and hurt. It was a miracle she didn't start any fires in her passage.

When she finally stopped her mad dash, she had to pull tight all that lovely heat. Yank it close lest she ignite the brittle pile of leaves at her feet. She slumped to the ground, hugging her knees, rocking.

Remembering that night.

"Come on, Janey. Don't be such a goody two shoes. Have fun for once."

"I am having fun." She held up the flask and took a

sip of the burning liquid. She wheezed as it scorched its way to her stomach, spreading a warmth that made her giggle.

"But you could be having more fun." He held up the white pill. "Two of these, and you'll be humming."

"I shouldn't."

"Lighten up, Janey. It's prom."

It was prom. One of the last nights she'd have as a kid. One of the last with Benedict before she told him they were breaking up.

"Okay." *Just this one time.*

The last thing she ever did as a teenager. The stupid act that led to her being a prisoner in her own mind for twenty years.

She'd be dead or in a coma still, if Adrian hadn't saved her.

He used me.

Saved me.

She couldn't help but remember how he'd gone out of his way not to take advantage. She was the one who kept throwing herself at him. And he kept shoving her away.

At least now she understood why, and it had nothing to do with his crappy excuse of doctor and patient not getting involved.

He feels guilty.

He was the reason she'd overdosed. He knew those pills were dangerous and never warned Benedict. But he wasn't the one who shoved them down her throat.

If she was going to hand out responsibility, then she needed to take some because no one forced her to do drugs. Benedict and others had asked her many times before, and she'd said no. Always said no. Except that one time.

The fact Adrian kept his mouth shut about their possible deadly effect was shocking, but not entirely surprising. She remembered how Benedict used to torture him. It was cruel and unnecessary. While she stepped in a few times, she only did so in front of Adrian. Out of sight, she was part of the problem, keeping her mouth shut. Sometimes even laughing at a rude imitation of a boy who never asked to be sick.

A boy who'd grown up to be a man. Handsome. Arrogant, yet with a core of vulnerability and a hint of wild. She could see it every now and then in his eyes, a barely contained primal nature. Because he'd cured himself using the same kind of weird DNA twisting as he'd done with her.

He was the reason she got a second chance at life, and while she could blame him for the pills, what would that accomplish? She could have just as easily been killed with Benedict behind the wheel. How many times had she let him drive her home high or drunk?

Letting her anger go, though, meant realizing she'd fled to the woods with only the clothes on her back.

She sighed as she sat on a fallen tree trunk. Now what?

There was no question Adrian would accept her back. He felt as if he owed her. But she didn't want his remorse. Nor did she want to paint the walls with his blood anymore.

Then what do I want?

Her body knew. It craved his touch.

Stop thinking like that. He's the enemy. The insidious voice in her head sounded so annoyed.

Which was weird because she'd long ago stopped thinking of Adrian as the bad guy.

If he's so good, then why are his ex-patients trying to kill him?

Because it could be confusing going from one state to another.

Stop making excuses for him. He deserves whatever fate those who hate him mete out.

Perhaps he did. But she wasn't one of them.

You're confused.

Maybe. She'd recently come out of a coma. She was different on a level human doctors could never comprehend. Who else could help her if she ran into trouble?

There are those out there you could join.

Like the shadow on the rooftop? The one who'd sent her in this direction looking for Adrian.

The question was, why?

The shadow did you a favor.

By sending her to the one man who could disarm

her? A man who, without hesitation, had shot someone who threatened him.

You wanted answers. You got them. Found out he is to blame.

For what? Really, she wanted to know because, while she might have been a little shocked when she first woke, lamenting her state of being, something had changed since then.

For one, she was fully awake now. Fully alive.

Alive and eager to discover. A miracle owed entirely to Adrian.

If not for his pills, you wouldn't be here.

Blaming the victim? She snorted aloud. That was crazy. She finally recognized that amidst it all. Yes, the pills were Adrian's, but he never asked to be bullied into giving them up. Didn't put them in her mouth.

He injected you with something far worse.

Did he? She smiled as she pirouetted in the forest, fingers trailing on the crisp fall leaves barely clinging to branches. They smoked at her passing. "I kind of like what I can do."

Who didn't dream of becoming a superhero? The strident screams of the vagrant and his crispy hand flashed in her mind.

You're no hero.

Okay then, villain. Did it really matter?

You are a freak in the eyes of humans.

The price of uniqueness. She would learn to deal with it. Adrian would help her if she asked.

Speaking of whom...

"Jane?" His voice echoed in the distance, loud and carrying. Stupid, too. Her head came up as she felt a stir in the environment, as if many eyes and ears suddenly took notice of the man that had walked into their midst.

The monsters who didn't thank him for what he'd done. She could feel their seething anger. Their craving for vengeance, waiting on their chance, and there he was, out here alone looking for her.

"Idiot," she huffed, while inwardly pleased. She'd half wondered if he would care.

Of course, he cares. He is a scientist. He wants to prod and examine you.

So long as he was naked doing it. For some reason, goading her inner voice into prudish silence amused.

How could two opposing minds live in one head?

Who says it's two?

Jane ignored the disturbing words as she concentrated on the forest around her. Given her skin prickled, she kept her inner warm core sucked in tight.

"Jane. Are you out here?"

Yes, you idiot. Stop yelling for me. The voice that time was entirely her own.

Did he not grasp how he drew those hunting these woods?

He knows. He doesn't care because he's worried about me.

Cared so much he'd probably die.

Unless she saved him.

She paused as she heard rustling. Adrian called again, close enough that she fixed on his voice and sought the shadows to find him. There. By the large fir. Wearing only a linen shirt and looking worried.

He called out. "Jane. Let me know if you're here."

Don't do it. He has a gun.

Once the voice said it, she saw it held loosely at his side, the muzzle pointing down.

She crouched, slowly lest he notice.

Adrian tucked his hands behind his back, hiding the gun, and stood still, head tilted to the side. Almost as if he listened. Perhaps he did. After all, he never did say what his side effects were.

What was he other than a mad scientist who appeared deliciously sexy with his rumpled hair? Although he'd be even sexier with his clothes off. Arousal coursed through her. Twenty years of pent-up frustration's worth.

A feeling, more than anything else, drew her attention upward. There in the tree towering over Adrian, something moved. A sinuous motion that overlapped many branches at once.

Adrian never looked overhead.

She coiled, ready to pounce.

The thing in the tree dangled down, quietly, arms reaching. Jane pushed with her feet to launch herself and...

Adrian never even looked. Just lifted the gun

and fired.

The body fell out of the tree. Jane finished standing and gasped.

"How did you—"

As Adrian turned to look at her, his gaze locking on hers, two more shadows barreled from between trees. One on each side. He could only aim at one.

She ran, knowing she wouldn't reach him in time. Adrian fired, hitting one of the bodies, leaving himself open for the other one. Before he could whirl, it slammed into him.

They went to the ground in a hard tussle. Shadow battled with darker shade. She could see very little as clouds passed overhead, vanquishing even the slightest hint of starlight.

But she could hear. Snarling. Snapping.

The rustle and breakage of brush. The meaty thump of flesh hitting flesh. The grunts of physical strain.

And I said, let there be light. She raised her hands as her mind did an imitation of a preacher praying. Her hands illuminated in balls of yellow fire. The forest lit, and she saw the strangest thing. A creature, very gorilla-like in the sense of its thick body covered in the darkest of hair. The features still quite human, not simian. But the long arms and bulky muscles, mixed with the slavering teeth, told the true story.

This is what happens when you give in to the voice.

The warning froze her only a second, and then she

saw Adrian underneath the monkey man, and the idiot wore a smile.

He turned his head and met her gaze, not paying attention to the real threat. Yet when that gorilla moved, Adrian's hands rose and held the other's neck, displaying strength.

Crack.

Ruthlessness, which was even sexier.

Adrian shoved the body off him and rose, brushing his slacks before bending to retrieve the gun.

"You don't actually need that gun, do you?" she accused.

He checked the slide then removed the cartridge and slammed it back in before answering. "Probably not. But I prefer to cover all the angles. I'll live longer that way."

"I highly doubt that. What possessed you to come into the forest? Especially at night."

"You already know why."

"I wasn't in any danger."

"You think I came to rescue you?" He arched a brow. "I'm fairly certain you can take care of yourself.

Her lips pursed at the unexpected praise. "Apparently not because I let Benedict talk me into something stupid."

"One act does not define," Adrian stated. "Now, a series of events, maybe then you can draw a conclusion."

"If that's the case, then, given all the stupid things

you've done, you're an idiot."

"Yes." He didn't deny. He did, however, smile, a crooked thing that made her heart pitter-patter faster.

Gag me with a spoon.

"How many of your patients are still running around looking to kill you?"

"Running around, oh about a dozen or so at least. But I don't think they all want to kill me."

She glanced at the bodies then back at Adrian pointedly.

He shrugged and offered a sheepish grin. "What can I say? I'm a popular guy."

She sighed and shook her head, lest she laugh. She knelt beside the gorilla man and perused him more closely.

"He looks like he belongs in a zoo."

"Now he does, but just a few weeks ago, Gary was able to talk and function just fine."

"What happened?" she asked.

"He escaped."

"You saying this happened because he skipped his meds?"

Adrian shook his head. "The actual medicine part is short. It's the recovery that takes time."

"How long did it take you?" she asked.

"I'm a bit of a different case," he said, hedging rather than replying. He knelt by the body of the serpent, more Lamia of legend with a human upper torso.

"Different how? You healed yourself with the same kind of treatment, right?"

"Yes. But at first, I had many different iterations of it."

"You look fine."

"For now. But I do have to keep a tight lid on it lest I slip and become something other."

"I don't change shapes, I think." Said with a frown.

His lips hinted of a smile. "No, you don't. For you, it's all about shaping heat."

"Less shape, more just brimming with it." It sloshed inside, a warm kernel that didn't mind being pulled out like taffy and molded to her desires.

"But you have to feed it," he said, placing something on the body before rising.

"Yes, I need heat. Fire works best." She pointed. "What's that?"

"GPS locator."

"Why?" I didn't make sense to have one.

"How else is the cleanup crew going to find the bodies?"

"Seems a waste of good meat." She eyed the serpent tail, wondering what it tasted like roasted.

"I have steak at home."

"Now you're talking my language." She began to strut away, wondering if he watched.

He passed her, eyes straight ahead.

It annoyed her. Especially since she was pretty sure his pretend ignoring was contrived.

She decided to test the theory.

"Brrrr. Is it much farther? I'm getting cold," Jane said.

"Shit. I didn't even think of bringing you a blanket or coat." Adrian glanced at himself, and his shirt. He'd rushed out without a jacket. He turned a concerned gaze on her. "How can I help you get warm?"

Adrian walked right into the trap she'd laid. Nearing him, she clutched his shirt and dragged him close. "I need you." She plastered her mouth to his.

"We can't." He struggled to turn his head. "You're my patient."

"You're fired. I'm going to find another doctor."

For some reason, that made him chuckle. "That might not be so simple."

"You're right. It's not. But if that's what it takes..."

He sighed. "I'm not right for you, Jane."

"I'd say that's my decision to make. Not yours."

"What do you want from me?"

Her lips curved into a mischievous smile. "You. Naked. Reminding me what it feels like to be alive."

"Jane." He moaned her name as he finally crushed her to his chest. His mouth hotly seeking hers. About time.

Their lips melded together in a searing kiss that sent blood coursing hotly through her body. She molded herself to him, enjoying the tight wrap of his arms. A shame they both wore too much clothing.

Something easily rectified.

She shoved away from him, loving how his eyes tracked her, glowing with passion.

A second later she glowed, too, as she exuded enough heat to send her clothes swirling away as ash.

"Jesus, Jane." Half plea, half prayer. He reached out, hesitated before touching her skin. "Will it burn?"

"I should hope so." She grabbed his hand and placed it on her breast. She wasn't a virgin, and twenty years had given her plenty of time to know what she liked. What she wanted.

He cupped her breast, squeezed it, found her mouth for a kiss as he kneaded it. It was rather easy, as it turned out, to tear the shirt from him, baring his upper body.

She delighted in the rub of her erect nipples against his chest.

His pants went next, shoved to the ground, and he stepped out of them, standing tall and naked before her.

Very erect.

She wanted to climb him like a tree and perch on his branch. But he had other ideas. He walked her backwards until she was propped against a tree. He then dropped to his knees, a supplicant before her, who lifted her left leg to place it over his shoulder. He turned his head and kissed the soft skin of her inner thigh.

She quivered.

He kissed his way to her sex, soft embraces that

brought shivers and moans. When she expected him to finally lick her, he instead ran his fingers over her honey-dewed lips, rubbing that moisture over her clit. The sensation had her arching her hips, bumping his face.

Her cheeks flamed with embarrassment, especially since he chuckled.

"Do you have any idea how much you excite me?" he asked, the words a hot flutter against her sex.

"Show me."

He did, his mouth latching onto her and licking. Not the inept act of a boy still learning to please, but a man. A man who worshipped her flesh. Who spread her lips with his tongue and lapped at her. Who grasped her clit with his lips and teased her.

Teased her so well she couldn't help but come, the heat of her climax making her glow. She remembered to keep it tight lest she burn him.

But he didn't make it easy. He kept licking her. Flicking her swollen button. Then shoved a finger inside her, drawing a gasp.

"More." Oh, how she wanted more.

"Turn around," he ordered. He rose behind her as she spun around. She understood his intent and grabbed hold of the tree trunk, automatically thrusting out her ass. She throbbed for him, her inner furnace hot and ready for his touch.

She felt him moving behind her, his hands palming her waist, arching her even further. He parted her thighs by inserting his foot between hers. The tip of his rigid shaft rubbed against her damp slit. Wetted itself in her honey. Teased her.

"Are you sure?" the silly man paused to ask, even as she knew he ached for this as much as she did.

"Very." She pushed back against him, sinking him between the lips of her sex, pushing him deep. Throwing her head back at the fullness that brought. The satisfaction.

It felt so good. He was so big. He throbbed as he remained still inside her. She felt him pulsing as if he held back.

Oh hell no. She pushed back against him, sinking him even farther, ground herself against him.

"Jane." Just her name. Groaned. And then he finally snapped.

He began to thrust, in and out, a driving, hard rhythm that soon had her panting as her nails dug into the bark of the tree.

The heat in her built as he kept slamming, the thickness of him stretching her. Pummeling her sweet spot in all the right ways. Ways she'd heard about, but never experienced until him.

"Adrian." Her turn to moan his name. To let him know she wanted him. Him and no one else. If possible, he grew thicker, and she got hotter. Enough that he exclaimed, "You're glowing."

And she was about to explode.

He must have known it, must have felt the heat,

and yet he kept pounding into her. Kept thrusting and pushing, his body slamming into hers until he groaned. "Not without you."

She didn't know what he meant at first.

He slowed down, curved his body to hers, drawing her upright. Her head leaned back into his shoulder. His lips latched onto her neck. His hands. One kneaded her breast, the fingers pulling and rolling a nipple. The other toyed with her clit. Rubbing and pinching while he ground himself into her.

A steady grind that had her hiccupping with pleasure, the inferno within growing hotter and hotter. His lips latched onto one spot, and he growled against her skin.

"You're mine, Jane." A claim that came with a firm bite of her flesh.

Enough to make her explode, the heat of her ecstasy bathing them. Binding them in a way nothing could tear asunder.

Unless you were a monster who thought it was a good time to interrupt. It came from the bushes with a scream of rage.

It met Jane's fiery annoyance.

She didn't leave anything for the cleanup crew to handle.

And Adrian...dear sweet Adrian...he gave her a crooked smile and said, "Want to share my bed?"

CHAPTER SIXTEEN

THE POUNDING ON THE DOOR BROUGHT A GROWL to Adrian's lips. He clutched closer the warm, naked body resting with him. But the interruption continued.

Bang. Bang. Bang.

Shaking off sleep, and the lethargy brought about by epic sex, he finally grasped the fact someone truly wanted his attention. It only belatedly occurred that none of his alarms had gone off.

Not a good sign.

"Shit." He rolled out of bed, leaving Jane under the covers while he grabbed for some pants. He pulled them over his ass a second before she said drowsily, "Honey, kill whoever that is, would you?"

Given how his cock swelled at her calling him honey, he'd gladly murder the person who was taking him away from her. He wanted nothing more than to dive back into that bed and make love to her until she scorched him with her climax once again.

But he had a feeling he wasn't getting any more rest—or sex—this morning, because sure enough dawn had come and gone. Entering the main living area, he noticed the sunlight streamed through the two-story windows that lacked the black-out curtains of his bedroom.

He rubbed his chest, the scratches a sign of a good time. He probably should have put on a shirt.

As he passed a console table with the basket of keys on top, he reached under and pulled the gun he'd clipped beneath it. After what happened at the old clinic, Adrian took to stashing weapons in every room of the house. Sometimes two.

He released the safety as he crept the rest of the way to the door with its insistent pounding. He tingled, awareness nudging him, danger spiking his adrenaline.

Should he call out? What if it were Jett? Or a delivery fellow?

Jett would have just walked in. He knew the keypad combination. The delivery guy would have dropped the package or left a notice by now.

So who did that leave? A home invader wouldn't announce his presence.

He stopped to the side of the portal, and the pounding stopped. Adrian waited, wondering if the person had left. His alarm system glowed green. Whoever stood outside hadn't triggered any of the motion detectors. He couldn't see, the only windows the transom over his large front door.

He still tingled, his being bristling with a sense of danger. "Who is it?" he asked on impulse.

"Me, you fucking idiot. Open the goddamn door!" Luke yelled, the sound of his voice muffled.

The panic, however, was clear. Adrian unlocked and flung open the portal to see Luke looming on his front stoop. "Why didn't you call to tell me you were coming?"

"I did," growled Luke. "So did Jett. You weren't answering. He's on his way."

"But you got here first." Meaning he'd been staying nearby.

"Yeah, I might have broken a few speed limits. It was an emergency," Luke stated.

Which could mean only one thing. "Where's Margaret?"

Luke jerked his head at the car. "She's panting in the backseat. Says the baby is coming. But it can't be. It's too soon."

"Not according to her body. Let's get her inside." Excitement hued Adrian's suggestion.

Luke held him back and muttered, "Before we grab her, you should know there's something wrong. She's in pain."

"Which is normal when going into labor." Adrian went to step past, but Luke wasn't done.

"I know normal, and I'm telling you something is

wrong. I think..." Luke paused. "I think the baby is hurting her."

"Then let's stop wasting time," Adrian snapped. He knew what Luke feared. Could almost smell it. Adrian just couldn't refute it. The baby was a hybrid. Who knew what the trauma of birth would make it do. Despite that, he offered reassurance. "Margaret won't die if I have anything to say about it."

"She better not, or you'll be seconds behind her," Luke growled.

A threat that Adrian didn't pay much mind. Luke wasn't the first father who panicked seeing his wife in pain, helpless to fix it.

Reaching the car, Adrian opened the rear door and saw Margaret hunched on the seat, knees pulled to her chest. Panting. Her damp hair stuck to her face in wet tendrils.

"Hello, Margaret."

She turned wide eyes on him. "Don't hello me. Get me inside and tell me you've got drugs."

"I've got a few things to help with the pain. Can you walk?"

"Yes." She went to get out of the car, only to have Luke scoop her into his arms.

"Put me down. I'm not an invalid," she exclaimed, only to gasp and cling tight to Luke as her body spasmed.

Luke's jaw tightened. "Basement again, I assume?"

He strode to the house, carrying his wife, without waiting for an answer.

As they entered, Jane appeared, looking tousled. "What's happening?"

"The baby's coming." He waved Luke on. "Get her in the bed. I'll be right there."

"She's going to deliver a baby in my bed?" Jane asked with a wrinkle of her nose.

"Is it still your bed?" he asked with an arched brow.

Her lips curved. "Guess not. Do you need my help?"

"I should be fine. Jett is going to be here soon with Becky."

"Then I'm going back to bed. I had a busy night." She winked before sashaying back to the bedroom, a view he wanted to chase, but Luke chose to bellow, "Are you fucking coming?"

It took but a moment to jog down the stairs. Margaret was sitting on the bed.

"Lie down," Luke ordered.

"Don't want to," she refused. She sat with her legs dangling, cradling her belly, panting.

"Give me a second to wash up and we'll have a look," Adrian said, heading for the bathroom sink.

When he re-emerged, Margaret immediately asked, "Did you get gas or needle for the pain?"

"I have both. Which do you want?"

In reply, she curved forward, rounding out her back. It made it easier for him to give her an epidural.

The needle slid with ease between the vertebrae, and the medication went to work immediately.

She uttered a sigh and said, "Thank God."

"That was fast." Luke sounded surprised.

"Which is why it's the method of choice," Adrian remarked. "Do you mind if we get you in a gown?"

She nodded, and Adrian immediately pulled the stack of freshly laundered gowns he'd had delivered. He handed one to Luke and then excused himself. He'd only had time for a quick wash before administering the epidural. He took a moment in the washroom downstairs to splash water on his face and change into some scrubs he kept there.

He wished he had time to pop in and check on Jane; however, Luke and Margaret needed him more than a sleeping nymph.

If she needed him, she could easily find him.

He exited the washroom to see Margaret now wearing a light pink gown. Luke held her hand, his anxiety probably not helping.

Time to see what they were dealing with. "May I check on the baby?" Adrian asked, indicting her belly.

Margaret lay down, and yet her stomach protruded, a mountain riding from her midsection. A jiggly mountain.

"The baby is active," he remarked.

"Baby's trying to pummel his way out," Luke muttered.

"It's probably agitated by the contractions. Not uncommon, I should add."

"She almost fell over walking he was rocking around so hard."

"Again, that kind of thing does happen." Adrian sought to reassure, and yet he needed to see what was going on. He flicked on the ultrasound, only to curse as the screen displayed an error message.

"What's wrong?" Luke asked.

"The system is insisting we run a software update."

"Then run it."

"I can't." Because, like his oddly misbehaving security system, his internet service appeared to be down. "We'll have to check on the baby using more old-fashioned methods. The good news is the last ultrasound showed junior with his head down. Here's to hoping he didn't flip."

"Pretty sure he's still head down," Margaret replied. "Feels like I've got a bowling ball hanging in my pelvis."

"Let's check, shall we." Adrian placed his hands on the taut skin of Margaret's belly, felt it ripple and lump as the child within moved. It made it hard to pinpoint body parts but, at the top of her belly, definitely a foot. "Still head down it seems. We should check on your cervix next."

But first, another contraction and, according to his watch, just over four minutes from the last. He felt the spasming as the uterus contracted, agitating the baby, who pummeled his mother, causing her to cry out despite the pain block.

"Luke, put a blood pressure band on her, would you?" he asked to give the man something to do.

While Luke jumped to obey—like a well-trained wolf—Adrian drew on new gloves and grabbed a small flashlight.

He looked at Margaret. "May I take a peek?"

"Any other man I'd kill," Luke remarked as she spread her legs and pulled up her knees, exposing herself.

But there was nothing sexual in what Adrian did. Childbirth was a biological thing. When he peered between her legs, it wasn't with sexual interest. When he placed his fingers within her, it was merely to check the progress of her dilation.

Which was poor.

He pulled out and snapped off the glove. "She's not even a centimeter dilated."

"Meaning?" Luke growled.

"Meaning, you might have panicked for nothing," Margaret relayed. "I'm still in the pre-labor stage."

"But you are having contractions. You're in pain."

Adrian felt sympathy for the man who wanted to help but didn't know how to fight. "Pre-labor is the beginning stages, and it can last hours. Sometimes even days." He faced her. "How long have you had the contractions?"

"About six hours now. But they were far apart until about an hour ago. That's when Luke noticed."

"You were in the bloody tub rocking. Fucking right I noticed." Luke had attached the pressure gauge, which started pumping and taking readings.

"Well, I'm certainly not sending you home," Adrian announced. "If your body is in pre-labor, then that means it's ready to give birth. The question is, do we wait and attempt a natural birth or do a C-section?"

"What do you mean attempt?" Luke growled.

"I told you before, the child is rather large. Margaret isn't."

Luke turned to Margaret. "What do you want to do?"

Rather than reply, her eyes rolled back in her head, and her body began to convulse. Her blood pressure dropped, making the decision for them.

"What's happening?" Luke cried out.

"I think she might be hemorrhaging internally. We need to deliver the baby now." He didn't mention the fact that he'd never actually performed a C-section. How hard could it be?

Pretty damned hard when the surface he needed to slice wouldn't stop wobbling. "I need the baby to stop moving," Adrian remarked. "Can you calm him?"

"By what, singing him a fucking lullaby?" Luke cursed, and yet he placed his hands on the rollicking tummy, which quieted. "That's a good boy. Let's stay still and let Doctor Frankenstein do his work."

Rather than protest the nickname—*I work with the living, not parts of the dead*—Adrian took a scalpel to the taut skin, hoping his research didn't lead him astray.

The blood was copious, gushing out of the opened uterus, along with the amniotic fluid that was left. A tidal wave that flooded the bed and dripped on the floor. To his credit, Luke remained standing, his expression pale but determined.

A fist found the hole and flailed free, the little fingers bearing sharp nails. Not claws, but still enough human-like enamel at the tips to have caused some damage.

"Impatient, fellow," Adrian muttered.

Beep. Beep. Beep. The machine indicated an ever-weakening blood pressure in the mother. He had to move faster.

Adrian reached into the flesh, fingers moving past stomach muscle and skin to grip the squirming mass within. He pulled forth the baby, who emerged with a mighty yell.

Junior yodeled with a perfect set of lungs, but Adrian had no time to admire him. "Cut the cord."

Snip. Luke quickly severed the umbilical, and Adrian thrust the baby at Luke, barking, "Wrap him." Because he had to save Margaret.

Blood still pumped from her stomach, and while Adrian used one hand to apply pressure, the other scrabbled for something to staunch the flow. A sponge was slapped into his palm, and he looked quickly to see Becky had arrived.

"She's bleeding out," he said unnecessarily.

A good nurse, Becky knew what to do. "Stop the flood while I get a blood drip set up."

Good thing he'd ordered a few pints.

While Becky got the IV going, Adrian dove into the uterus, which was the source of the problem. The baby had shredded it. In places it was almost ribbons. There was no time to ask.

It all came out. Once it was gone, it was a much easier task to stop the bleeding then stitch Margaret up, the scar larger and uglier than it should have been. But Adrian had something to fix that.

Only as he stepped back and uttered a sigh of relief at the stable beep of the monitor did he notice Jane had joined them. She stood watching as Luke handled the baby. The swaddling not exactly tight, which meant parts of the blanket flopped.

Becky bustled around, setting up more monitors for Margaret and another IV for fluids.

Luke eyed him, too afraid to ask.

"I think she'll be fine, but unfortunately, she won't be having more children."

The statement made Luke's eyes shimmer, the green fire rolling over them and disappearing. "But she'll recover."

"She should. The bleeding stopped once I removed

her uterus. I've had Becky apply a balm that will aid in the healing."

"You better not have given her one of your treatments," Luke growled.

"This is perfectly safe, I assure you. Now"—Adrian held out his hands—"let me see him."

For a moment, he thought Luke would refuse. But he ended up handing over the child, and Adrian felt a moment of awe as he stared down at the hastily wiped face.

Having been born via C-section, the baby didn't have the strange cone-shaped head often present in vaginal births. It was round. Big. Probably too big to have come out naturally. The eyes were open wide and inquisitive.

"Hello, little man," Adrian murmured.

The baby fish-mouthed him and kept watching.

Adrian stripped the blanket and gently placed the child on a scale.

"Thirteen pounds seven ounces," he announced. He then measured the length. A very sizeable twenty-three inches. The baby didn't cry as Adrian inspected him, rather regarded him with startling green eyes. None of the cloudy blue common in regular newborns.

"Is he okay?" Luke asked.

"So far he's better than okay. Top percentile for his age, a score of ten on the Apgar. Congratulations on the birth of your son."

Jane drew near as Adrian stepped aside to allow

Becky—crooning softly—to place a diaper on the baby, one that she had to adjust due to the projecting tail, a few inches long and covered in a soft down. But it might have been the full set of teeth when the baby grinned that sent Jane fleeing from the room.

CHAPTER SEVENTEEN

Running out of the room probably gave the wrong impression. Yet what else could Jane do?

When she saw Adrian holding that child, staring at it with such warmth, she felt a stabbing urge—

Need.

Want.

—for them to have a child of their own. Which was crazy.

Look at the pain and suffering Margaret went through. The child tried to rip its way out of the womb. So much blood. Damage.

If not for Adrian, the chances of the human woman surviving...

But Jane wasn't human. She could handle a little roughness if it meant having a kid. What about Adrian, though? It was one thing to create monsters in others, but did he want one as his firstborn? Or would it be an experiment to him?

The expression on his face as he looked upon that child, though, wasn't avarice or even scientific inquiry, but awe.

Which was exactly how a person should look when confronted with a fresh, new life.

You're just seeing what you want to see. Adrian is evil.

The whisper in her mind surprised, mostly because she thought she'd come to terms with him. Might even be falling for him.

Foolish girl, falling in love with a monster.

If he was a monster, then what did that make her?

He needs to die. You should kill him, urged that insidious voice.

The very suggestion of it brought a frown. Why would she kill Adrian? She owed him her life. And after last night, she was more than ready to give him her body.

Whore. Stop thinking with your cunt. Go back there and kill him. Kill them all and take the baby.

Steal someone else's child? The very idea was repugnant. And yet it whispered again.

Take the child. They don't deserve it.

It was in that moment she realized the voice wasn't her own. And hadn't been for a while.

"Get out of my head," she snarled aloud.

Go ahead and make me. I'll bet you can't. You'd first have to find me.

The taunt was inside her. She raised her face to the sky and yelled, "Leave me alone."

Why, when you're so much fun to play with?

Again, the words teased, but she wasn't amused.

Who screwed with her head?

The last person you'd suspect.

How long had someone been messing with her mind?

And how could she stop it?

You can't.

"I'm not killing Adrian, or anybody else," she boldly declared.

Then you're of no use to me.

Ominous words. But even more ominous was the prickling of her nape.

She whirled, hands rising and filling with fire, which did nothing to stop the darts that struck her.

She screamed in rage, "Who dares?"

I do. Shhh... Sleep.

The drugs in her system spread lethargy through her limbs, and her lashes fluttered. "No," Jane managed to mumble before she sank to her knees and knew no more.

CHAPTER EIGHTEEN

IT TOOK A WHILE BEFORE ADRIAN WAS DONE IN the basement. He monitored Margaret until she woke, dopey eyed but managing a smile when Luke presented their son.

She managed to drink down some reinforced broth —with a bit more of the military-grade healing agent he'd sold to the Russian government for a pretty penny.

He'd run every test imaginable on the baby. Junior passed them all with flying colors. Adrian didn't say anything to Luke—worried he might freak—but he knew Becky noted the fact the child was much more advanced than a newborn should be. It would be interesting to see if the child aged more rapidly than an unmodified child. Just like he was waiting to see if any other traits would manifest.

Luke had at least calmed down, probably due to

Jett bringing down a bottle of booze and insisting on a toast.

"To your son," Jett declared with a glass held high.

"To another Chimera secret," Luke added with a twist of his lips.

"He'll have some friends soon enough." Jett cast a glance at his wife's belly.

Hopefully there would be many babies. Adrian knew better than to mention his concerns, yet he remained all too aware Becky's pregnancy progressed nothing at all like Margaret's. Their children would be vastly different. However, now that they'd managed one successful birth, he worried more than ever about those who'd escaped. Would they begin procreating in the wild? He wasn't too concerned about them mating with the beasts. What if, though, one of his more volatile patients managed to impregnate a human woman?

The risk to the mother, as evidenced in this birth, was much higher than usual. But that wasn't the biggest concern. They'd gotten lucky Junior was born with only a tail to differentiate him. The next new generation baby could be born with a fin or horns.

Worried that's what your kid will look like? taunted his inner voice. *Maybe some hooves for the son of the devil?* The laughter didn't help his state of mind.

When Margaret's eyes drooped again, Luke declared she needed her rest. Before they all traipsed upstairs, Adrian had Becky set Margaret up with a breast pump, the suction pulling at her leaking nipples. With luck they'd fill a few containers with milk. Breast-feeding might be recommended by pediatricians; however, Margaret took one look at her son's full set of teeth and shook her head. "Like hell is he coming at my boobs with those things." The decision was made to bottle-feed but with breast milk, if she could supply any.

Peeling off his gloves and changing his bloody coat for a fresh one, Adrian took one last peek at the child.

Junior slept in the incubator, more a precaution than necessity given his temperature was perfect. Everything about the baby was perfect from his ten toes and fingers to his steady heart rate and excellent hearing. He even had the neck control to turn and watch when he heard a sound. Unlike most newborns, he didn't have a glazed look in his eyes. He stared and focused. Recognized his mother and father and reached for them.

But being born was tiring work, and now Junior slept.

Becky stared down at him. "Will my babies be born this big do you think?"

Standing alongside her, Adrian shrugged. "Doubtful given it's twins. You, of all people, should know each pregnancy progresses a little differently. What is true in one is not necessarily in another."

"I'm worried," she softly admitted.

"As am I," he said, not able to lie to her. "But rest

assured I will do my best to ensure everything goes smooth."

"It's kind of scary to know I'm going to be one of the first mothers to a new generation of humans."

She had good reason to be afraid. Had Margaret not come to him when she had... Luke would be a devastated man right now.

But Adrian didn't say any of this. Instead, he chose to reassure. "You'll be fine. This birth, the first of many, is cause for celebration. You might be looking at the end of suffering for all of mankind."

"Or the beginning of the end," Jett remarked, coming close. He pointed at the baby. "What are you going to do about the tail?"

About four inches in length, and covered in a soft down, it emerged from the base of Junior's spine, just above the buttocks.

"I'd say that's up to Luke and Margaret." But personally, Adrian thought the child should keep it. Change should be embraced.

Becky went quiet for a moment, most likely to gather her thoughts before saying, "What if my babies don't come out looking human? Or they can't live outside of water?"

"Then we will create a place for them to grow where they won't come to harm."

"What he means to say is cage them." Jett glowered darkly.

"It doesn't have to be cages," Adrian corrected. "It

all depends on how they behave. Which kinds of falls back on you. With the funds I've got in an offshore account, we can create a compound, a place where all those who are different can live in peace, protected from the outside world until they are ready."

"Or they go nuts." Jett remarked.

"You calling me crazy?" Becky retorted, slapping him in the arm.

"You're the one dipping frogs in melted peanut butter before eating them." Jett's nose wrinkled.

"Says the man who eats powdered cheese puffs made of so much artificial stuff there's no actual food in them."

The banter, good natured and full of affection, showed how a couple should be. Could he ever get that with Jane?

As Jett wandered off, speaking in a low murmur to Luke, Becky sidled close and muttered, "Is it me, or are you steadier these days?"

"A bit."

"Is it because of Jane?"

Becky knew of Adrian's theory that mating helped ground those who were losing their grip. He shrugged. "Could be. Could also just be that I've remembered who I am. What I am."

"Which is?"

"An imperfect being who loves medical science but still requires the companionship of others lest I forget the true reason a doctor should heal."

Becky blinked at his strange statement. "In other words, a mad doctor with friends."

"In essence."

Becky smirked. "I'm going to tell Jett you like him."

"I didn't say that."

"Say what?" asked the man himself as he rejoined them, leaving Luke to clasp the hand of his sleeping wife.

"I was saying we should let the new father and mother get some rest. I have a feeling Junior will keep them busy." Adrian grabbed hold of the incubator and rolled it closer to the medical bed.

Luke turned tired eyes on him, which brightened at the sight of his son. "Thank you."

Sincerely said and possibly even finally forgiving.

Adrian's throat tightened. "I'll just be upstairs if you need me." He left the basement with Jett and Becky, in dire need of the bar upstairs and a slug of something that burned on the way down.

Only after his glass was refilled did Adrian finally sigh and lean against the credenza. Jett sat on the couch, Becky snuggled at his side. Only Jane was missing. Probably gone back to bed.

As if she'd stick around for you, boyo. She probably ran far and fast.

So what if she did? He was done making choices for people.

You should care. She's dangerous.

Yes. She was. One of the reasons she drew him. As

to finding out if she was here or gone... Time enough to discover it. He had more pressing issues now that the baby had been delivered.

He broached the security system issue. "You could have warned me you were taking the security system down to let Luke in."

Jett frowned. "What are you talking about?"

"Didn't you shut it off?" Adrian straightened. "I assumed you'd done it remotely since Luke called you first."

"Done what exactly? I punched in like normal when I arrived."

"You might have, but I didn't get any notifications. Doesn't appear as if any of the outdoor sensors are working. System was lit up in green lights, and yet Luke managed to make it up my driveway in a car and right to my door without a single alarm going off."

"Impossible." Jett sprang from the couch and headed for the laptop on the desk. After a few minutes of typing, he pointed at the screen. "According to this, everything is active and functioning."

"Let's test that, shall we? Check the log and see if it registered you arriving." Adrian tossed back another shot of booze and then refilled, unable to halt a glance down the hall at the closed bedroom door. Was she snuggled in bed? Naked perhaps...

If yes, why the hell was he still out here?

He set the glass down. "I think I'm going—"

"Fuck. Shit. Mother humping piece of garbage." His usually placid right-hand man cursed a storm.

"Speak to me, Jett. What happened to my security?"

Jett's lips turned down. "The system's been hacked hard. From what I can tell, it's just running green lights and empty video feeds of previous days. It's a sophisticated scam."

"In other words, not a glitch." Adrenaline returned to push the fatigue away. "We should get ready."

"For?"

"Attack. Obviously, someone wants us vulnerable."

"Don't you think they would have attacked before now?" was Jett's dubious reply.

Adrian shook his head. "No, now makes the most sense. They know the baby's been born, the mother stabilized. Everyone is tired and relaxing. It's the perfect time to make their move."

"Who, though?" Jett asked.

"Doesn't matter. Something is coming. Grab what you need and get yourselves ready to leave."

"Where are you going?" Jett asked as he Adrian moved toward that closed bedroom door.

Tick. Tock. He'd soon find out if she was behind it.

"I'm going to get dressed. Give me a second." He entered his room and was glad no one was there to see the disappointment that surely marked his face.

The bed gaped emptily. The sheets still rumpled, the faint hint of sex still in the air. No Jane.

She's gone, boyo. She hates you.

He wouldn't believe that.

The bathroom door loomed wide open. The glass on the shower door showing it empty. Still no Jane.

You should have chained her up. Like a dog.

No.

Why not? You did it to everyone else. For their own good.

The words stung with their truth. *I only ever wanted to help.*

And yet he kept sending people running from him. Those that returned just wanted to kill him.

Not everyone. Luke was downstairs and had trusted him with his child. Jett and Becky had never left his side. Even Jayda had convinced Marcus that Adrian wasn't too bad of a shit.

But those were only a handful of people who didn't want him dead.

Your enemies are legend. The snide cackle only pressed his lips into a grim line.

Adrian strode to the sliding patio doors leading from the master bedroom to the upper deck. Perhaps she'd gone outside for a breath of fresh air. A glance outside showed the patio empty. The propane fire feature cold.

She was gone.

Adrian returned to the bedroom and quickly dressed, a cable knit sweater over his upper body, fresh slacks, warm socks. Exiting his room, the first thing he noticed was the mighty frown on Jett's face.

"Shouldn't you be loading Becky into the car?"

"I've got the keys. We can leave anytime. We've got a bigger problem."

"What's wrong?"

"Someone hacked the security system." A statement that lacked a climax.

Adrian arched a brow. "You already told me that."

"Yeah, but I didn't realize to what extent. They've been watching this entire time. Since the moment you moved in. Still watching even now, I'll wager." Jett looked at the camera above the door leading outside. There was a camera by every single entrance. Only the bathrooms and master bedroom lacked them.

Someone with that kind of access would be aware of every single move he made. Every word he uttered. All the secrets.

So many, many secrets.

"That's fucking bad." He glanced down at the floor as if he could see Luke and his family through it. "We need to wipe as much as we can and go into hiding."

"Do we dare move Margaret, given what she went through?" Becky asked.

"Don't have a choice, Red," Jett answered for him. "We can't stay here."

Adrian's lips pursed. "She should be fine. I'm more concerned about getting out of this area unmolested. We have to assume the hacker is watching the roads."

"If you're right, and they're planning to attack, then they'll have people positioned along it."

"The woods, too," Adrian surmised, glancing toward the sliding glass door.

"That's insane," Becky muttered. "You're talking about a huge-scale operation."

"We have to assume it's huge because that way we'll be better prepared." Adrian pushed at Jett and began tapping at the keyboard.

"What are you doing?" Jett asked as Adrian's fingers flew.

"Hacking the hacker." While he'd specialized in medicine and biology during university, he'd supplemented his income playing with computer code. There was something soothing about machine language. The formulas. The strings and functions that he could manipulate. "First, let's take back control of my cameras." A process which started with severing all outside connections and then bringing the various zones on line, one at a time.

"What makes you think the hacker won't just take over again?" Jett asked, pacing behind his chair. He'd moved Becky away from the windows. A sound precaution, as was the gun he'd placed in her hands.

"They might, but it hasn't happened yet."

"What makes you think that?"

"Because I'm pretty sure they wouldn't want us seeing this."

The driveway showed a pair of SUVs, not even

making an attempt to hide, parked blocking in Luke's car and slanted across part of his garage.

"How many guys?" Jett asked as he checked the magazine on his gun.

"Unfortunately, I can't rewind to see how many got out, but I doubt both vehicles were packed. Assume four per, eight in total."

A deadly chill froze Jett's expression. "Not for long."

Becky held her hands over her belly. "You might have an advantage. If they're here for us, then they want us alive. which means they're probably armed with tranquilizers."

"Most likely, but just in case they aren't, shoot to kill." Adrian didn't plan to leave anyone alive. Already, too many people knew his secrets.

Jett cast a glance at the bedroom door. "Where's Jane?"

"Gone." Adrian didn't elaborate because then the screaming voice inside might finally escape.

One of the small video screens showed movement. A body creeping around the side of the house, edging toward the sliding glass door to the basement.

Adrian headed for the stairs. "Get ready to hold this level."

"Where you going this time?" Jett asked with exasperation.

"Downstairs to arm Luke."

"You're gonna give the wolfman a gun?" Jett

snorted. "Just when I think my life can't get any weirder."

Adrian left him behind as he jogged downstairs, barely hitting the bottom step before Luke stood bristling in front of him, his eyes glowing with primal green fire.

"Gonna shoot me, Adrian?" Luke snarled.

"We have company."

Instantly, Luke went from bristling to serious. "Who?"

"Does it matter? I'm pretty sure you don't want to see Junior put in a cage."

"Not if I have anything to say about it. Point me in a direction."

"And leave the baby—who is probably their target —unguarded?" Adrian asked.

As if knowing he was mentioned, the baby stirred.

Luke glanced at the child, then Margaret, then Adrian again. "Fuck me. This just complicated."

"Not really. Take Margaret and the baby into the bathroom. Guard them. I'll handle the guests."

"You?" Luke snorted. "This isn't a lab where they're strapped down and at your mercy."

"I'll have you know we rarely tie down our patients during treatment. It's afterward that things get a little hairy."

"Understatement of the year," Luke muttered as he scooped a drowsy Margaret and carried her to the bathroom. Adrian had just grabbed the baby when he saw something from the corner of his eye. He turned his head and couldn't miss the man outside the window pointing a gun at the glass—just recently replaced since the incident with Jane.

The weapon fired and barely managed a dent. But bulletproof glass was only so durable. The guy began shooting over and over, mocking their misassumption that the invaders wanted the inhabitants of the house alive.

"That guy is starting to really piss me off," Luke snapped, grabbing the baby from him.

"I'll be sure to let him know when I confront him. Close the door." Adrian shoved Luke and pulled the portal shut.

He then drew his second gun. It made him think of a meme, a dirty one, that said real men double fisted.

The guy in the window still fired away. Overhead, came a *pop pop pop*. Jett was having issues of his own.

The assailant at the door stopped firing for a second, but it was only so that a voice from outside could shout, his words amplified by some kind of speaker. "Surrender now and no one has to get hurt."

As offers went, it sucked. Surrendering would put them all in cages for sure. Adrian didn't think he could live in a cage.

The voice yelled again. "Hand over the pregnant mermaid and the child and the rest of you can go free."

An even worse deal. Did this idiot seriously think they'd agree?

"Like fuck." Which meant they'd have to fight.

Adrian lifted his gun and fired, right in the weak spot, which was paler than the rest of the impact streaks. Then he fired quickly again and again until the bullet finally went through the hole he made, right into the guy standing there.

Hold on, make that the guy lying on the ground. One down. At least seven more to go. Maybe six since Jett would kill at least one. Adrian headed for the door and hit the code to allow him outside.

He no sooner stepped out than someone shot. Given the furrow it left in his bicep, it was a bullet, not a dart.

But that was the only shot as someone yelled, "If you kill the doctor, we don't get a bonus."

Attacking for money. Something he could understand. Which was why he stepped out further and dropped his guns before he lifted his hands. "I don't suppose anyone wants to make a deal. I can double whatever is on the table."

"You ain't got no money left, Dr. Chimera." A man emerged from the corner of the house and placed a hand on the shoulder of the shooter. The rifle was still aimed at Adrian.

' "More than you might think. I've got hidden accounts."

"Nice try. But you'll have to do better than that. We're here to take you and all your guests in."

"I thought you just wanted the pregnant one and baby? Change your mind?"

"Those are the most important two. The rest are just additional bonuses."

"Who's paying you?" Adrian asked. He took a step forward, hands still overhead. The rifle jerked at his movement, but the fellow didn't shoot.

"Stop right there, Chimera."

He halted and tucked his hands behind his back. "You have to know this isn't going to end well for you. Didn't they tell you what happened at the farmhouse?"

The fellow with the craggy features didn't react. Then again, given the massive scar bisecting his face, could be he suffered nerve damage. He certainly suffered from stupidity.

"You can't scare us. You're outmanned and outgunned."

"Again, didn't they warn you what happened at the farmhouse?"

A sneer pulled the lip only partially. "Yeah, we heard. You sent in your monsters to kill everyone in the place."

"Actually, it was one man. Marcus, to be precise. They took his girlfriend, and he decided to take her back."

"Can't have been one guy." Scarface shook his head. "There were seven dead on that mission."

"One. Man." Adrian repeated, his fingers wrapping

around the grip of the gun he kept tucked in the waist-band of his pants.

"You're not that man."

"You're right, I'm not. But Luke is." Adrian ducked as he whipped out his gun.

Two hundred and fifty pounds of wolfman soared over his head and slammed into the rifleman. They went down in a tussle that involved much growling and a set of screams that ended abruptly.

As for Adrian, he pivoted and fired behind him. The sneaky soldier dropped. Adrian then aimed over-head and heard screaming as his shot went through the wooden deck into someone's foot.

"Surrender, or I'll shoot," screamed Scarface, the gun in his hand steady as Adrian strode forward.

The idiot wasn't scared yet.

You'll have to try harder, boyo.

"Who sent you?" he asked.

"Bite me." Scarface fired, but Adrian moved fast. So fast, he didn't have time to blink as the barrel of his own gun angled and he pulled the trigger. He hit Scarface in the leg, sending him to the ground cursing.

At least he didn't blubber and snivel. He took his wound like a man.

"Fucking asshole. They told me you were a pushover."

"It is really bothersome to me that my enemies think me so weak." Adrian crouched by the man, hand dangling the gun. "Do you think I'm weak?" He fixed the guy with a stare.

"You're insane," spat Scarface. "And sick. I know what you're doing. You and your monsters."

"That's a shame because then that means you know what I do to people who might spill my secrets."

"Go ahead and kill me," blustered the guy.

"I will, but first tell me where Jane is."

"Who the fuck is Jane?"

"Hot redhead. Sometimes throws fireballs."

The man smirked, a lopsided thing that angered Adrian. "Your girlfriend was the first one we nabbed in the woods. She's back at our headquarters by now I'd wager. You should join her."

The fact that she had been captured provided a slight elation. Maybe she'd not left him after all.

"Where is she?"

"Come with me and you'll find out."

"I said, where?" Adrian pressed the muzzle of his gun against the man's forehead.

Scarface continued with his arrogant smile. A face so like Benedict's that Adrian lost his temper.

He was wiping his gun on the dead man's shirt when Luke came loping at him from the woods, sporting epic sideburns and hair even Wolverine would envy.

"How many did you get?" Adrian asked.

Luke flashed five hairy fingers. Plus, the two on the

ground courtesy of Adrian. There couldn't be many left.

"I'll check on Jett. You peek in on Margaret and the baby."

They split up, Adrian taking the outside stairs to the upper level of the patio, seeing two more bodies on the deck. And another three in the house standing across from Jett, their bodies lightly swaying, as if hypnotized. Perhaps they were, given Becky sang, her hair lifting and dancing around her head, her voice lilting and rushing, inviting and calming.

Adrian's entrance startled her and halted the song. The men snapped out of it. One reached for Becky and died when Jett shot him. Adrian shot the second, as for the third...

Once they captured him, that soldier told them everything they wanted to know—which didn't amount to much other than the address of the warehouse where they'd taken Jane.

Adrian only hoped he wasn't too late.

CHAPTER NINETEEN

WHEN JANE REGAINED CONSCIOUSNESS, IT WAS TO find herself sitting on the concrete floor of a warehouse. The high ribbed ceiling with girders and the towering containers kind of gave it away.

Her clothes exuded a smoky scent. As a matter of fact, there was a distinct smell of burning meat in the air, as if someone had a barbecue.

Uh-oh. What happened while she was out?

A glance down at herself showed her clothes intact, if dirty. She appeared unharmed. Untethered, too.

She stood and looked around, noticing the vast warehouse stretched a good distance and was set up maze-like with stacks of shrink-wrapped pallets. They were of less interest than the body to her left. The charred remains still smoked, the fat crispy, making her stomach rumble. Past the body, at the far end of the aisle formed by towering product, a door.

Freedom! She began to walk toward it when the shadow from the rooftop stepped in front of her, an indistinct blob that drawled, "And just where do you think you're going?"

Without thinking, Jane drew fire to her palm and flung it. Only to miss as the shadow darted to the side.

"You throw like a girl," it taunted.

Jane held on to her next fireball. "Who are you? What do you want from me?"

"I wanted you to kill Chimera, but you didn't listen to me."

She recognized the plaintive tone of the voice she was used to hearing in her head. "It was you planting ideas in my mind."

"Not so much planting as cultivating ones that were already there."

"I don't hate Adrian as much as you do."

"You should because he made you just like he made me." The shadow gestured to itself. "I only exist because of him. He played God. And now it's my turn to play executioner."

"So why kidnap me?" Jane asked, pacing left. The shadow kept pace with her. She stopped when her back was to the door behind her.

"Since you won't kill him, I guess I will. And what better bait than the pussy he's slamming?" The shadow crossed its arms.

"What makes you think he'll come to my rescue?"

"Pleasssse," the shadow said with a raspberry S. "That guy is so in love with you. He would never let his poor Janey-waney down." The mockery dripped thickly.

Yet Jane found a strange elation in the idea Adrian loved her.

"Why do you hate me so much?" Jane cocked her head, trying to pierce the shadow clinging to features that somehow seemed familiar.

"I don't hate you. I pity you. You fell for his bull-shit. Fell for the guy that made you into a victim. There's a name for people like you."

"Forgiving?"

"There is no forgiveness," boomed the shadow.

"You have a beef with him, then by all means take it up with Adrian. But don't think you can use me in your vendetta."

"Oh, but I already have."

"You won't get out of this alive," Jane stated. She was beginning to suspect she was the reason for the bodies on the floor. She'd spotted a second charred corpse between the stacks.

"If I die, you're coming with me."

Jane quirked a brow. "Was that meant to be a proposition? I already have a boyfriend, thank you."

"Chimera is a killer."

"So am I." But in a strange twist, Adrian proved to be the one person she had no interest in ending.

There was a clang as of a door opening. Startled, Jane glanced over her shoulder to see Adrian striding into the warehouse, his hands spread. "Jane! Are you all right?"

"Adrian!" She beamed, only to frown. "Don't come any further. I don't want the shadow to get you."

"Too late, Janey."

Jane faced the shadow being. "Leave Adrian alone. He hasn't done anything bad."

"Other than supply the pills that led to you losing a promising future."

"I made that mistake," she spat. "He didn't make me swallow those white pills."

"Um, Jane," Adrian interrupted. "What are you doing?"

"Trying to save your life," she retorted with a hot glance over her shoulder.

"From who? There's no one here other than corpses."

"What are you talking about?" She stepped aside and pointed. "The one who's been whispering bad things to me is right there."

"I only see you."

"Look again."

"I am," he replied softly. "Maybe you should, too."

She looked down and saw her finger pointing to herself. "I don't understand."

"I guess it's maybe a bit late to ask if you've been hearing voices."

"Yes. I thought I was going crazy."

"You're not. It's a side effect of the treatment. I hear a voice, too."

A frown knotted her brow. "You mean, all this time, that shadow and voice were me?" She shook her head. "That can't be right, because it keeps telling me to kill you."

"Actually, that tends to be very common as well. Becky says it's because it is engrained in humans to hate the creator of monsters."

"I'm not a monster." She tilted her chin.

"None of us are. We're just different."

"Different is another word for crazy." She paced, glancing at the charred body then her hands again. "How do I get rid of the voice?"

"You don't. Just ignore it. It's what I do."

"Does it work?" she asked.

"Most of the time." He shrugged. "You learn to tune it out eventually."

"But it's a part of me." She touched her ribs. "Surely there's a way for us to exist as one."

"It would mean fully embracing your other half. And you've seen how that usually ends up." He referenced the monsters from the woods. Mindless things who'd not joined with their other half so much as given up.

"Becky embraced hers."

"Becky is a special case, and I should add it hasn't

been that long. We have no idea about the longer-term effects of giving in to the other side."

"What about Luke?"

Adrian's lips pursed. "He's also a special case."

"Or are they the answer? What if I said yes to my voice?"

"You risk losing yourself."

Her lips turned down. "But don't you see..." She swept a hand to showcase the burnt remains. "I already have."

He reached for her. "Let me—"

There was a thump, as if something hit the roof overhead.

She raised her eyes. "Did you bring reinforcements?"

"Just Jett, but I left him by the car once I saw the bodies."

"There's more outside?" Of course, there were. She had a vague image, a flash of men screaming as they jumped out of a vehicle.

"What about Luke and the others?"

"I left him behind to guard the women and the baby."

More thumping overhead. "I don't suppose Jett likes to pretend he's a gargoyle."

"He might scowl like one, but he doesn't sit on roofs."

"I think we're in trouble." So much trouble and they were out of time.

The men burst in from everywhere, their combat boots smashing through the skylight windows. Ropes dropped down, quickly followed by men rappelling. On the floor level, more trouble arrived, at least a dozen men, if not more, attacking.

Unfair. They had guns and numbers. They wanted to hurt her. Hurt Adrian.

Putsss us in a cage, precious. She didn't understand the strange cackle, but she did grasp this wasn't a time to hold back or be squeamish.

She let the rage rise in her, her inner voice surfing the wave of heated anger. Her temperature rose and pooled in her hands. She held up a palm, which ignited with fire, orange with licks of red and yellow. She flung a ball of it at a rope, where it stuck, melting the strands, sending a body plummeting with a scream that cut short.

More men were coming, more than she could handle at once. But Adrian was here. He didn't fear as he stood tall and took aim.

Bang. Bang. Bang. She didn't have time to see if he killed all those he shot at. She tried to keep up with the bodies rushing her. Did her best to defend against the bullets. They sheared past, nicking her skin, letting her blood flow in molten rivulets.

Opening her mouth wide, she let out a primal cry and blew fire. It poured from her mouth in a liquid stream that brought screams, and panic.

It was beautiful. And hot. She sucked in all that

delicious warmth. Would have taken it all in, but she didn't. She wanted her enemies to burn. They sizzled as they died. Screamed until the flames sucked the air out of their lungs.

More. More fire. More!

The voice demanded, but it wasn't the only one striving for her attention.

"Jane?"

Turning on feet that no longer touched the ground, she stared without seeing. Held her hands out and ignored the screaming in her head—*This isn't me. I'm not a killer!*

Yes, she was. This was her time.

Her place.

And there was her enemy. Right in front of her.

"You," she said in a deep voice. "Must die."

"If that is the price for Benedict stealing my blue pills, then so be it." He knelt in front of her. Dropped his gun yet he didn't bow his head. He held her gaze. "But I know my Jane doesn't want me dead."

"Jane's not here." The lips quirked, while, within, the other Jane screamed about sharing and forgiveness.

"Then you might as well kill me. Because life isn't worth living without her."

He bowed his head and waited for her to act.

She lifted a hand that dripped with blue flame. The color caught her eyes, and she stared at it.

Blue pills.

That wasn't the first time he'd said that. The truth hammered at her rage.

Hammered at her reason for vengeance. Hammered so hard she never heard the one invader she'd missed.

The bullet hit her in the chest.

CHAPTER TWENTY

THE BULLET HIT JANE. BLOOD BLOSSOMED ACROSS her chest. Eyes wide in surprise, she went down. Whereas Adrian dove for his gun and rose with a snarl. He shot the man who dared, too late.

Jane lay on the floor and didn't move.

She's dead. The woman he'd loved for twenty years. The only one he'd ever wanted. Dead because he didn't save her.

His mind shattered, and he roared, ***"How dare you!"***

The exclamation vibrated the very air.

Kill them, the voice whispered. *Kill them all.*

Because he could hear more of them coming. Their whispers like shouts. Their stench offensive.

Let me avenge you, boyo. Set me free.

Not free. Not entirely. A partnership.

You do realize you bargain with yourself? mocked

the voice.

Adrian knew. He'd always known it was just easier to pretend the voice was someone else. He didn't want to face the fact that it represented a primal part of him. A savage side he didn't want to acknowledge.

Fact was he was a monster all along. It just took the treatment to be honest about it.

Let's see what I can do. Adrian spread his arms wide and closed his eyes. He expected it to hurt, to, at the very least, tingle, and yet when he hit the ground with hands that were more like paws and a jaw with more teeth than usual, he felt...greeeeat!

The tail at his back swished, and look at that, he even had wings. A true chimera, just like his name, with all the power he needed for revenge.

There was something to be said about killing without the use of a gun. The sense of closeness shared with a prey as you pounced and pinned them to the floor. The exhilarating rush as hot blood filled your mouth. The euphoria as you inhaled their last breath.

He especially liked it when they tried to fight. It made tasting their defeat all the sweeter.

Because he was a conqueror. All powerful. Majestic and unstoppable.

All too soon there was no one left to kill. Only then did he roar again, finally taking note of the injuries that bled on his body. The exultation of battle faded into sadness. So very, very sad, enough that his adrenaline evaporated and his body shrank back to his original shape. He knelt beside Jane's prone body and clasped her limp, yet scorching hand. The heat of it almost burned his flesh, but he didn't care.

A shudder of grief bowed him, and Adrian laid his head against her belly. Her shirt smoldered against his face as if the heat within her body sought to burst free.

Or did it heal? Because, to his surprise, the ear he had pressed to her felt a soft flutter as if from the faint beat of a heart.

Which seemed impossible. The bullet had torn through her chest. The blood—so much blood—pooled around her on the concrete floor.

"Jane?" He glanced at her face as he spoke her name softly. Her features held a serenity, her eyelids closed with her lashes brushing her cheeks. A faint curl of smoke wisped from a nostril. He stroked a finger down her cheek—and yelped.

"Jeezus you're hot." Hot enough to blister skin.

The hand he held began to scorch, and he released it and leaned back, noticing the air shimmering around her, making her porcelain skin glow. Was she about to self-combust?

She'd yet to move. Or even draw a breath he could see. The ragged hole in her chest had stopped bleeding and now smoked. All of her oozed a hot steam, and she glowed brighter.

Adrian rose to his feet, his clothes flapping in tatters. Perhaps he should stay. Immolate in the cleansing flames with her.

But then it was as if he could hear her voice.

Take cover you, idiot.

He didn't question. Rather he turned on a heel and ran, ran for the door exiting the warehouse, knowing he probably wouldn't make it.

Says who, boyo? The challenge only made his legs pump faster. He bolted straight out the door and had made it a few yards when it happened.

The boom of the explosion rattled the very air and trembled the ground underfoot.

A wave of heat blasted him off his feet, and he hit the pavement outside the warehouse hard. For a moment he lay there, kissing the pavement, the pain in his bruised body indicating he lived.

He groaned as he rolled to his back, noticing the sky glowed, lit by the flames shooting from the remnants of the warehouse. Nothing so mundane as orange and red but white-hot flickers hinting at a bit of blue. The hottest a fire could get.

When Adrian managed to regain his feet, he could only stare in grief-stricken awe at the raging inferno. All those who'd attacked, cremated, along with his special Jane.

I failed her.

He'd waited too long to embrace his inner beast. Waited too long for so many things. Like telling her how he really felt. As a scientist, he should have mocked the idea of love at first sight. Then he'd met Jane. A woman who'd touched him with her mere presence. No other woman could compare.

No other woman ever would.

Because I'm perfect.

The voice he heard even had her feminine intonation, which brought a frown.

Now that I've made peace with myself, will I forever be haunted by her?

Such melodrama. Again with the sassy remark. It sounded so much like Jane.

Because it's me, idiot.

He blinked in disbelief as she emerged from the inferno, hips swaying, the shape of her absolute naked perfection. And very much alive.

She reached him, and he sputtered, "I saw you get shot." Yet not a mark showed on her chest.

"Yeah. That part sucked." Her lips quirked. "Which is why I had to combust. For some reason that fixes everything."

The geek in him breathed, "Just like the phoenix, rising from the ashes."

"More like reborn in fire."

Sirens in the distance had him frowning. "We need to get out of here."

Not what he wanted to say, and yet, he didn't want to stick around and attempt to explain to law enforcement what had happened here.

Jett leaned against the car parked on the road and shook his head as they approached. "Couldn't you have put a shirt on her at least? Becky's gonna flip if she finds out I saw another woman naked."

"Shit." Chagrinned, he pulled off his ruined sweater, only to have Jett sigh. "Take mine instead." Jett handed his jacket to Jane. She slid it on and was covered to mid thigh.

They got into the car, and as they pulled away, Adrian could only hope this was the end of their problems. Probably not, given he doubted the mastermind behind the hacking and attacks was in that warehouse when it blew. Which meant they still might not be safe. "How's Luke and his charges?"

"He got the women and kid to the safe house I had set up a while back."

"Because you didn't trust me," Adrian remarked.

"Because I don't trust anyone," Jett offered with a smirk in the rearview. They went silent for a second as a fire truck screamed past, lights flashing and siren wailing.

"They're safe, though?"

"For the moment. What happened back there?" Jett asked, his gaze flicking to Jane, who leaned against the seat, lids closed.

Her eyes opened to show a kaleidoscope of color. "They all died."

Adrian snorted first. "Yes, they did, but they weren't all Jane's kills. I took out my fair share, too."

"Who were they?" Jett asked.

Adrian shrugged. "I still don't know. But it's obvious they'll stop at nothing to capture us."

Which meant they couldn't stick around this city, and once they reached the safe house, they delayed discussing their options, given Becky and Margaret were sleeping.

But Adrian couldn't avoid it when Jane chose to follow him to the basement where Jett finagled a cot for him.

"You should get some sleep," he suggested. "It's going to be a long few days getting out of the country and covering our trail."

She stood in front of the stairs—the only way out—with her arms crossed. "You're thinking of leaving."

"Hmmm," he said, turning his back to her lest she see his face. "I don't know what you mean."

"I mean, you're planning to wait until everyone falls asleep, and then you're going to sneak out."

"As if Jett's going to sleep." He couldn't keep avoiding her gaze.

Her head canted to the side. "Why are you leaving me?"

The urge to lie was right there. Instead he sighed. "Because we can't be together." Much as he wanted to. Much as he loved her.

"Why not? I think we already ascertained the fact I won't burn you to a crisp in bed." Her lips quirked.

The reminder brought an erection, but he also strengthened his resolve formed during the drive to rescue her. "I've brought you nothing but harm. You've seen firsthand the death and destruction that follows me. I'm the reason you were in a coma. My pills put you there."

"What color were those pills?" she asked.

"Why does it matter? I'm the reason you almost died."

"It matters. What color were they?"

"Blue."

"Are you sure?"

He shot her an annoyed glare. "Of course, I'm fucking sure. I took them for years to control my tremors. Right up until I cured myself."

"The pills Benedict gave me were white."

He blinked. "Are you sure?"

She snorted. "What do you think?"

"Then they weren't mine."

She shook her head. "Nope. All this time you've been feeling guilty for something that wasn't even your fault. And I was mad for the wrong reason."

She stole some of the wind from his sail, but being a man, he knew how to be stubborn. "Even if I'm not at fault, I need to go. You deserve a chance to discover the world. Meet people."

"I can still do that by your side. Haven't you gotten it yet? I know what I want. Who I want." She grabbed hold of his shirt and yanked him close. "I want you."

"But—"

Rather than listen to more protests, she sealed the deal with a kiss. Sealed his fate with her touch.

Gave him what he wanted but, for the first time in his life, feared taking.

With a groan of surrender, he slanted his mouth over hers, joining their lips, the passion between them heating. As if it needed much to ignite.

Arousal heated all the blood in his body and left him awash in sensation. Every nerve ending in his body hummed. Desired. He throbbed with need.

She nibbled at his lips, her demanding sucks making him part his mouth that their tongues might duel.

He held her tight to him, his fingers gripping her by the hips, pulling her snug against his frame. He could have cursed the layers that separated them. She still wore Jett's jacket, and someone had scrounged a pair of track pants for her. All impediments that he spent too many seconds stripping that he might touch her. Feel her.

Skin to skin. And the burning he felt? Came from within.

He was too frantic for niceties or foreplay. Lucky for him, she was just as eager. She shoved him down on the cot, which creaked alarmingly, especially when she clambered on top of him. But when he thought she would ride...

Instead her head ducked, and her lips latched onto his swollen head.

He almost bucked her off the cot. As it was, he had to grip the edges of it tight as she sucked him, drawing him deep into her mouth. The suction was epic. The heat of her mouth scorching.

But not as hot as her sex. He dragged her toward him lest he finish in her mouth. He kissed her, sucking on her tongue, his hands on her hips guiding her to his cock.

Her nether lips spread to take the tip of him. Then all of him as she sat down hard.

They both gasped. Stilled. Enjoyed the moment of intense sensation. He started rocking first, moving his hips in a motion that pushed him deep, and he was rewarded with a clenching of her channel.

She panted as she dug her fingers in his bare chest. Shivered, not in cold but passion, a shiver that went right through her and fisted him tighter.

He kept grinding, and she rocked with him, pushing and rolling, her pleasure triggering his.

He whispered her name as he came, but she shouted his as she lit up like a candle.

A moment of glory where he beheld her with her, a curvy woman with a hint of smoky red and gold phoenix wings, riding him, loving him. Joining them in a way no one could ever tear asunder.

Leaving him limp on the cot.

But ready to go when she said, with a smile so impish, "Now that we got that out of the way, let's do that again more slowly."

Slowly led to the fire alarm going off, which led to red cheeks—on his part—and a promise to tone it down.

When Jett left—threatening to shoot him if he woke them up again—Jane giggled. "I think your man is jealous."

"What makes you say that?"

"Because you made me come so hard I literally set the house on fire."

EPILOGUE

"This sure beats the snow in Canada any day." Jane kicked happily at the hot sand, probably the only redhead in the world who could walk in full sun on a beach and not worry about burning.

"Don't get too used to it. We can only stay here a few weeks before moving on." Always moving. It was the only way to thwart their enemies.

"Moving on doesn't mean we have to leave the Caribbean," Jett remarked from his spot on the towel under the umbrella, hogging the shade. He kept watch on the waves, where his wife swam with the dolphins, her belly big and round.

"It's too hot," Luke complained, his nose smeared in a white blob of sunscreen. "And Maggie won't let me put the air conditioning temperature down in our room because of the baby."

"Good lungs on that boy," Jett remarked, which

caused Adrian to snicker. They'd all heard the yelling at three a.m.

"I was heating his bottle fast as I could." In the interest of being an active parent, and helping Margaret recover, Luke had taken over the middle-of-the-night feedings. He was still adjusting to having a son who turned rabid when he got *hangry*.

"Maybe you should ask Chimera to create a treatment to give you a milk teat," Jett laughed

The suggestion brought a glare from Luke and a snarled, "Keep giggling it up, big boy. You've got two of them coming."

The reminder sobered Jett.

Adrian defused the situation before it got too tense. "Hey, good news. The babies finally turned human in the womb, eh?" He'd begun to wonder if Becky truly would birth a fish or frog. However, the last ultrasound showed two perfectly formed girls, causing no end of amusement in Becky when Jett started pacing and talking of expanding his gun collection.

From the direction of the villa they'd rented—cash —strode Jayda, who'd joined them not long after they fled Canada. She kept walking even as she shaded her eyes to take a peek at the surfing Marcus. The guy had excellent balance and the right kind of gold locks for beach bum. Whereas Adrian always looked uncomfortable—because the damned sand always ended up in his pants.

Turning from the ocean, Jayda made her way to

them, her expression grim. As soon as she got close enough to speak without yelling, she announced, "My dad's finally surfaced."

"Yet your expression doesn't seem happy," Jane noted. "Is he injured?"

"Nope. Although he will be once I get a hold of him. He's talking to the press and telling them all about Chimera's secrets."

Which wouldn't end well...for any of them.

THE FOLLOWING SPRING...

Grass had already begun to creep over the rubble left behind by the clinic. If Oliver had not known its location—received via an informant—he might have never found it. It certainly didn't exist in any databases. No permits were issued for its construction. The land was technically owned by the crown.

Yet for years, a mad scientist had experimented on people in this spot. And not just Adrian Chimera— now missing, hopefully dead. He'd had an army of employees all sharing his vision. Some of them even sharing in the treatment like that Doctor Cerberus, who'd gone public with what they'd done.

Fucking monsters. Those involved not just geneti- cally monstrous but depraved due to their actions, too. Taking innocent people, some without the ability to speak for themselves, and conducting medical tests that were inhumane. Changing them into something else. A few of those poor patients had been recovered. Caricatures of humanity—with a thirst for blood.

All because of one man. One sick, sick man.

But Chimera was out of business now. On the run. Possibly dead, depending on the rumor you listened to. His staff, those that remained, had scattered. Their names and locations unknown. The world ignorant of what they'd done.

Not for long. He planned to expose the evil. But for that, he needed proof. The notes and pictures he'd taken of actual patients had disappeared. Wiped clean off his computer as if he'd imagined it.

Which left only one option. The clinic itself.

It wasn't easy to reach. He didn't dare hire a helicopter. That would mean telling someone else before he was ready. He did it the hard way, driving as far as he could with an ATV then hiking. Hiking for days.

However, the grueling trek proved rewarding when he crested that last pass between the mountains and beheld the valley he'd been searching for.

The lake, the remnants of an oval track, a concrete pad used for helicopters. A pile of rubble where a building had once stood.

But the true prize was discovered later that night when he began going through the images he snapped at sunset.

He almost missed it, but something strange caught his eye as he scanned the pictures. He pinched his screen to zoom in. The enlarged image made even less sense.

In the shot, Oliver saw a girl, or so it seemed. Her features were delicate, eyes huge, peering at him from behind the hump of the old clinic.

He swiped to the next picture, too blurry. The next, there she was again, with her big elfin eyes.

And projecting from her forehead...a fucking horn.

HELL YEAH, WE'RE GOING THERE. ARE YOU READY FOR *CAPTURING A UNICORN*.

For more books by Eve Langlais or to receive her newsletter, please visit EveLanglais.com